Death Comes to Hel...............

&

Other Stories

Amanda M Arnold

Published by and available from
theendlessbookcase.com

Printed Edition

This booklet is available in a variety of formats both paper and electronic.

The Endless Bookcase Ltd
71 Castle Road, St Albans, Hertfordshire, England,
UK, AL1 5DQ

ISBN: 978-1-912243-52-5

About the Author

Amanda grew up in North London and after leaving school and college she spent several years working in the fashion world in London.

Relocating to Norfolk she has enjoyed living near to the coast and her interests include art, photography, entertaining and travelling abroad. These topics often find their way into her fiction.

Also by Amanda M Arnold

The Humptons

The Humptons is an entertaining tale of the inhabitants of two rival villages. It follows the lives of a number of the village members including the rumbustious titled owners of an ancient estate, a butler and his eastern mail order bride, several upright ladies and some not so upright, a professor, an artist and even a retired Brigadier.

The book makes for perfect light reading and has a fun, entertaining atmosphere to it. The Humptons takes a fond look at life in a village community, touching on the many happenings and relationships that take place in a rural setting. However, it is not all sweetness and happiness, darker events play their part too in a disappearing way of life.

A Bolt Hole for Zelda

Romance has gone stale with no indication from Zelda's partner Donald to commit to their relationship. Deciding to put the eight years they've spent together and the life of luxury she has become accustomed to behind her, Zelda sets off to Cornwall after receiving the news of a property that's been left to her under very mysterious circumstances. With few possessions and her two Red Setters in tow, Zelda proceeds to investigate in an attempt to discover who left her the property and why.

After meeting an attractive man who is filming a documentary of the local area, Zelda finds a new relationship starts to blossom between them. However all is not as it seems in this quiet coastal beauty spot and with her new friends and challenges, some troublesome times lurk around the corner...

Full of twists, this romantic novel is perfect light reading that will keep you guessing.

Contents

Death Comes to Hellham Creek

'She didn't!' Prue gasped!

'She jolly well did.' Aurora's voice was cold with contempt.

'But her attempts at writing are pathetic, I mean having a dig at you a professional author it's ---Prue's voice trailed off as she stirred her coffee and shook her head in disbelief.

They were sitting in the cosy Tearooms in Hellham Market on a misty autumn morning. 'Yep, she told me she never reads chicklit! To be honest, I don't think she has any idea what that is, she just wanted to be nasty.'

Prue short for Prudence, a name she thought her mother had chosen in anger because she really had wanted a boy, absentmindedly buttered her teacake while she digested this latest information on the despised Miriam.

'I wouldn't have minded so much if she had ever shown a glimmer of talent at the writers' group. Completely without any idea of how to write fiction and with no imagination, her pieces are pants.'

Aurora shivered. 'Someone on my grave darling.' she said by way of explanation. 'Miriam is not worth bothering about, a blot on the human race and not very human at that. Do you know she dropped my lovely rainbow opal ring that I bought when I was in Australia? I collect big rings and that ring is the biggest. She asked if she could look at it, then whipped out the jeweller's magnifying eyeglass she carries in her handbag. After twisting the ring this way and that, she gave me a direct deadeye look and let my newest pride and joy smash onto the tiled floor. Miraculously it survived but

1

you could tell from her expression that she was disappointed. How nasty was that?'

'Appalling,' a concerned Prue said thinking that Aurora had gone deathly pale. 'Miriam also tried to break up your relationship with some of the group by saying that you thought everyone's stories were rubbish. A cheek from someone who mostly has an excuse for not producing a home story because she realises it highlights her lack of talent.'

Suddenly Aurora said, 'Did you hear that? How very odd. An ice-cream van playing Waltzing Matilda.'

Prue had heard nothing and now was even more concerned about her friend however; she decided it would be best to pretend that she had, so nodded in agreement.

'Not the sort of tune they usually play', she lied, 'and rather late in the year for ice creams.'

They chatted on however, Aurora was obviously still seething at the behaviour of Miriam, a recent arrival in the village and a fairly new member of the local writers' group.

To change the subject Prue smiled and fixed her very green eyes on a still subdued Aurora. 'Tell me about your trip to Australia darling. Was it fun, how did you get on with your cousin?'

'Oh, Tony was lovely. He showed me a lot of the area round where he lives on the Western Coast. The beaches are fabulous, and we drove further up north to see the more remote towns.'

'It sounds wonderful, I have always wanted to go there, and their wine beats all the others.'

Just then, a very loud siren sounded and came to an abrupt stop. They both glanced out of the bow window and saw people running past and stopping in a crowd outside the teashop. The flashing light of an ambulance cast an intermittent beam on people staring down at someone lying in the road.

'Come on let's go and see what's going on.' Aurora said, picking up the bill and going over to the cash desk. Having paid they joined the crowd of onlookers outside and gazed down at the figure lying motionless in a large pool of blood, their legs splayed out in an undignified tangle. The white face was familiar.

'Good grief it's Miriam!' Prue gasped.

A Paramedic turned on hearing this.

'Do you know this lady? What is her name?' He said, getting out a notebook as the other medics loaded Miriam onto a stretcher and into the ambulance.

'Yes, her name is Miriam Mills and she lives with her husband at the corner house in Shore Road, Hellham Creek, the village where we also live and that is how we know her.'

'Thank you, that is a great help. Your friend is in a bad way, but we will get her to the hospital and they will do all they can. Try not to worry.'

'We won't.' Aurora whispered in Prue's ear, then seeing the ashen faced and shaken looking driver standing by his dented car, said to a Police Officer taking statements from witnesses.

'How did it happen?'

'It seems the lady walked straight out in front of the car without looking. Witnesses say she appeared to be in a kind of hypnotic trance.'

The officer resumed his writing as they walked back to Prue's car.

As Prue drove the short distance back to Hellham Creek, Aurora said, 'What shall we do about telling Ernest? He will not be home until after about six o'clock.' Ernest was the Pharmacist working at a chemist in Marsbury Magna, the nearest sizable town.

'I will phone him about seven and if the police have not made contact already, tell him that his other half is in the local hospital.'

'Okay, do let me know how Miriam is darling; she looked in a bad way.'

Aurora waved as Prue drove away, and then opened the door to 'Tideways', her lovely house built many years ago, overlooking the misty creek. The Dutch gables at both ends of the roof were distinctive. They reflected the time when Flemish workers came over to build the long bank to stop the sea flooding the rich pastureland. Vast reed beds on the land side of the bank were home to many rare birds, whose calls rang out from dawn to dusk. When it was low tide, it left mudflats, topped with blue sea lavender and bright green samphire. Myriads of small creeks ran between the chunks of slippery, shiny mud, home to crabs and wading birds.

The house had been in the Graydon-Boles family for years and they used it mainly for holidays and weekend getaways. Now Aurora wrote her books there in an upstairs room that overlooked the creek. She was usually alone in the house on most weekdays as Henry Graydon-Boles, QC, her husband, worked at his chambers in London and only joined her for the weekends. They also owned a large white colonnaded house near Regent's Park where Henry stayed during the week. In summer friends or family came to visit

Tideways and the house was a riot of boating gear, cricket paraphernalia, kites and wet swimsuits. The washing machine would churn away, filled with many loads of mud-covered clothes, while the smell of wet dogs filled the hallway.

Merle, Aurora's younger sister would arrive for visits in her large S U V complete with her many children and faithful Nanny on board. As Merle emerged from the driver's seat, either she would have a new baby bump or Nanny would be clutching the newest arrival. When quizzed as to why she did not have children, Aurora would reply that Merle had enough for them both. The truth was she realised that she did not want to be distracted from her writing.

Merle was married to Marc the lead guitarist and vocalist of a famous rock group, who were often on world tours. They had met when Marc had spotted a straight-out-of-school Merle in the front row at a London concert. After a whirlwind romance, a pregnant Merle had bowed to her shocked parents' wishes and tied the knot just before Star was born.

When Aurora tutted at the announcement of yet another baby, Merle shrugged and said, 'I am just so pleased to see Marc when he has been away for months.'

Merle and Marc were often pictured in the gossip columns of newspapers and glossy magazines as they posed on the red carpet at music awards ceremonies. Merle was still in her twenties and prettier than all the female stars lining up for photos.

At seven o'clock Aurora phoned Ernest.

'Hello Ernest, have the Police been in contact?'

'Oh, Aurora I am so glad it is you. Yes, they have just left, and I am about to go to the hospital to see poor Miriam. Please will you come with me?'

This was the last thing Aurora wanted to do, however, she could hardly refuse.

'Of course, Ernest, I will leave now and meet you there. Try not to worry, bye.'

When Aurora arrived, Ernest was waiting. They took the lift to the third floor and followed the sign to the Intensive Care Unit. When they entered the big airy room, to give Ernest a chance to talk to the consultant, she wandered over to the row of four beds. The only sound was of the artificial ventilation pumps as they blew air into the motionless patients' lungs.

Miriam was lying in the second bed covered by a single sheet. Tubes snaked out from under the sheet and one was attached to a drip entering her neck as well as a large tube in her mouth. The regular noise from the ventilator timed with each puff. Miriam's chest quickly rose and then slowly subsided until the next puff.

Not knowing quite what was expected of her Aurora gazed down at the pale face. 'Hello Miriam.' She said quietly.

Miriam's eyelids flew open but only the whites were visible, then the lids came down again. A shocked Aurora stared around however, no one else had seen this. Perhaps I imagined it she thought although she knew it had happened.

Ernest finished talking to the consultant and nursing team then joined Aurora at Miriam's bedside.

'They say there is no hope, poor Miriam is brain dead. It is up to me when they turn off the ventilator. It is a terrible decision to make. In addition, they have asked me to give permission to donate her organs. As one of her closest friends what do you think?'

'We were not really that close Ernest, I only knew Miriam for a few months since you moved to Hellham Creek.' Aurora replied, not wanting to be involved in such a decision, 'did you not discuss what to do if one day it became an issue?'

Ernest turned tearful eyes to Aurora. 'No, I suppose we thought we were too young for it to be important. Yes, you are quite right it must be my decision.'

Aurora squeezed his hand. 'I will leave you now Ernest. I am sure whatever course you decide to take it will be the right one.'

With that, she took a last look at Miriam and left Ernest gazing at his comatose wife.

Arriving back at Tideways, she was surprised to see Henry's car parked outside the house. Running up she threw herself at her startled husband and clung to him until, laughing he gazed down at her and said, 'What a welcome, can I assume you are pleased to see me.'

'Oh Henry, I have just come from the hospital. Miriam Mills has been in an accident and is on a life support ventilator. I have never seen how that works before and although I disliked her, it was so eerie. Do you know, when I said hello, her eyes opened for a second and only the whites showed, it was horrible?'

Henry nodded and said quietly, 'That must have been a reflex action or perhaps just an electrical impulse. I have heard of that before when I have been in court. I am afraid though it is most likely she is brain dead.'

Pulling herself together Aurora looked up at him and smiled. 'I am so glad you are here, but why? I thought you were not coming until the weekend.'

'Let's go inside and then I'll explain.' He said, leading the way into the house.

Once they were in the sitting room Henry went straight to the cocktail cabinet, and poured out two stiff gin and tonics.

'Now sit down darling and I will explain.'

Aurora loved the calm way Henry dealt with any problem. They sat side by side on the sofa and after a long pause, while he savoured his drink Henry began.

'An extremely violent criminal that I prosecuted for the Crown and who was sent down with a long sentence has escaped, I have been warned that he has sworn to kill me. Unfortunately, he knows of the two places where we live so I have come back in case he turns up here.'

Aurora drained her glass and held it out to Henry.

'Refill please Henry, it has been that sort of day. Do you really think we are in danger?'

'Well, we'll hope for the best but still take every precaution. These old lags do often seek revenge however, we will make sure that the house is as secure as possible. I have told the police and they say to contact them if anything suspicious occurs. Now let's have something to eat and hope our criminal is all talk.'

'Ok, I have some spaghetti bolognese and garlic bread in the fridge that I can stretch to two. While you are checking that everything is all locked up I'll pop the food in the oven.'

'Good girl.' Henry said going into the hall and putting on his jacket. Then with a large torch, he went out through the back door and into the garden, returning several minutes later with the shotgun that he kept in a locked cupboard in the tool shed.

'All correct outside,' he reported, 'I have checked the security lights are working so there is nothing more we can do.'

After the meal, Aurora loaded the dishwasher and turned off the kitchen lights saying as she stifled a yawn, 'Let's turn in now, it has been an eventful day and you look exhausted.'

Later in the dead of night, Aurora woke up with a start and heard a metallic scraping noise. Heart pounding, initially she froze, then nudged the sleeping Henry who immediately sat bolt upright.

'Can you hear that? I think someone is trying to break in' she whispered.

They crept down the stairs and saw a dark shadowy figure of a large man outside the patio doors. Using a hefty screwdriver, he was trying to remove the door handle and lock.

Henry banged on the glass and shouted several swear words. The startled would be intruder dropped the screwdriver and ran up the garden, outlined in the bright moonlight. As he ran, there was an intermittent whoop— whoop—whoop— sound and an object flew through the air followed by an unearthly shriek of pain and the man fell motionless to the ground.

Opening the patio doors Henry stepped out into the garden then turned around to Aurora. 'Will you be all right if I go and see what has happened, darling?'

'Just a bit shaken but don't worry about me just be careful, that man may still be dangerous.' She replied in a shaking voice.

'Good girl, now you phone emergency services and ask them to send a police car and an ambulance crew as quickly as possible.'

Within five minutes, the place was swarming with burly police officers in high-vis jackets and paramedics kneeling on the grass beside the prostrate figure of the badly injured man.

'Most odd.' Inspector Musgrave, the senior police officer said to Henry, 'this is definitely Mick Stein the escaped prisoner you were warned about however, what caused his catastrophic injury is unclear. There is no weapon we can find so what caused this mighty blow to his neck is a mystery. You say you and your wife were watching from inside the house and that you did not see anyone else in the garden?'

'That is correct,' Henry replied, 'just a weird noise and we think we saw an object flying through the air.'

The paramedics lifted Mick onto a stretcher and as they carried him away, he began to try to say something.

'Hold on a minute, what is he saying?' Inspector Musgrave bent over the dying man trying to decipher the word, and then shook his head, 'Carry on, I cannot make any sense of it. He keeps repeating one word that sounds like mat something.'

'Look at this sir,' a young police officer said, pointing to what looked like a pile of sawdust, 'most odd, although it has been raining it is bone dry.'

The senior police officer pulled a plastic bag out of his pocket and scooped up some of the dust saying, 'I will get this analysed.'

When the ambulance had driven away, one of the police officers went back to the house to take a statement. Then finally, Aurora and Henry were able to sit in the kitchen with a cup of tea. The sun was coming up and dawn was breaking.

'What a night, it is tomorrow already. I am glad that is over, and we are still in good shape unlike Mick Stein.' Aurora remarked with a yawn.

Just then, the phone rang, and Henry lifted the receiver.

'Oh, hello Inspector, what is the news?' After a one-sided conversation Henry nodded and said, 'Thank you for letting us know, goodbye.'

Hanging up the phone he sat down and took Aurora's hand, 'Mick Stein is dead, his neck was broken, and the hospital has confirmed that the blow from a blunt instrument also ruptured a main artery. They have no idea what the blunt instrument could be. All very mysterious.'

Life calmed down after that and it was the day of the writers' group's monthly meeting. The members took it in turns to host the meetings and this month it was at Peaches Frost's converted barn. Seated round the table were the other four female members and Roger Blackett the only man who had been brave enough to join them.

Peaches gazed around, and her smile was tight and serious. 'Welcome everyone. First, I expect you have all heard of the sad accident that happened to Miriam, the newest member of our group. Our sympathy goes out to her husband and...' She then realised there was not really an and. Her voice trailed off then continued in a determined fashion, never one to dwell on negative issues, 'shall we start in the usual way by reading our home stories?' It had been agreed not to call the stories they wrote on a given subject homework as that made them sound as if they were still at school. 'Roger, you start.'

Irrespective of the given subject, Roger's stories always involved a war somewhere. It was a topic that he loved however, the girls did not. They listened politely and there was a murmured 'very good.' when he finished.

Although now retired, Roger had been the Personal Private Secretary to several Foreign Ministers and therefore, involved in many tricky situations with other countries. He never wrote about real events, but his tales were quite gory and featured spies and despots.

The meeting progressed with the reading of the other members' stories and then it was time for the midmorning coffee break.

'Hands up those who would like tea.' Peaches said counting hands, 'now coffee.' Numbers arrived at, she went into the kitchen to inform her mother, who always came in to take the strain if it was a social event. Peaches was a clever girl who had been spoilt by her parents and played up to it by acting helpless.

'She needs a lot of help'. Her mother would say as she ran around fetching and carrying.

'Thank you, mummy.' Peaches said as her mother staggered in with the loaded tray and then ran back to the kitchen to return with a tin of homemade biscuits.

As they helped themselves to the biscuits, the first topic of conversation was about Miriam.

'I know someone in the hospital and they say it is only a matter of time before Ernest will have to let them turn off the ventilator' remarked Roxanne who was an amateur mystic and excelled in predictions of the future, romance and death. It was uncanny how accurate she was and her tent at local charity festivals was always busy.

'Do the police know yet how the criminal who was trying to break into your house died Aurora? I mean have they found the weapon?' Roger peered over his glasses at Aurora and wiped a biscuit crumb off his moustache with a paper napkin.

'Not yet Roger. However, they are waiting for an analysis of a substance that was found near Mr Stein which may provide an answer.'

Lottie, sitting next to him was always amazed that criminal lowlifes were generally referred to as Mr. 'I gather he had been in and out of prison most of his life.' She said, not wanting to be left out of the conversation, 'It was very lucky he did not get into the house.'

'Very lucky.' Aurora acknowledged, 'He was a big brute of a man.'

They all murmured sympathetically and put their empty mugs on the tray, which was quickly whisked away into the kitchen.

'Thank you mummy.' Peaches said shuffling her papers into a neat pile. 'Now for our exercise today, write a paragraph on the senses. Make a list of what they are and then describe in what context you would use them.'

There followed much deep thought and then only the sound of pens scratching on paper broke the silence. After ten minutes, they took it in turns to read out their efforts. As usual, there were long pauses while they tried to understand their own scribbled writing.

After Peaches announced that the topic for the home story was to write a romantic tale the meeting broke up. Roger thinking he could write about a sort of James Bond type spy who rescues a lovely girl from an evil despot.

All the members lived within walking distance of each other. Lottie walked along with Roxanne until they came to her whimsical house, made by knocking two old cottages into one fair sized house. The brass doorknocker was of a fox. The bell pull a black, springy curl of metal, a jangly domed bell hung from it and at the side of the door was a copper nameplate inscribed with the name Bait Diggers Cottage. A previous owner had added a glass windowed balcony in the front. This looked out over the creek and was lovely and warm even when the east wind blew over the mud flats. Roxanne would sit there with her binoculars and watch the many birds that came to feed at low tide.

Now widowed, she had been married to a renowned professor of ornithology. She had joined him on his research expeditions to distant lands around the world. It was on their travels that she had studied the black magic rituals or voodoo ceremonies of many sects and tribes. This was the knowledge that she brought to the various readings she gave.

Lottie and her husband, Eric, a well-known chef, ran a B and B at their house called The Moorings on Smugglers'

Quay. It was the only place to stay in Hellham Creek and was booked up all year round. They had won many plaudits and a couple of trophies when they took part in the TV programme where owners of guest houses tried to outdo each other to be the best. Three other couples who ran B and B's arrived armed with cotton wool buds, sticky tape and a magnifying glass in the hope of finding signs of dust or rogue hairs in the beds. At The Moorings, they always failed.

However outlandish the competing pairs tried to be with their orders at breakfast Eric was never fazed. In fact, he welcomed the chance to dish up the perfect poached egg on toast and his Full English was unbeatable.

Their daughter Mu, short for Muriel was not quite the full shilling. Sweet by nature, she was obsessed with cleaning and polishing. Each day she attacked the whole house with an array of sprays and polishes. Every surface shone, every window gleamed, each bathroom sparkled and smelt like a greenhouse full of highly perfumed blooms.

When Mu finished her housework, she would take their big Doberman called Prince and walk the couple of miles along the bank to the beach. She would run along laughing at his antics as he jumped the waves. Lottie never worried about Mu if they were together. Prince guarded Mu fiercely. It was as if he knew that she was vulnerable. No one would get near to her unless he let them. This gave Lottie time to sit at the computer in the office and write. She had already published two cookbooks that were based on Eric's recipes and was halfway through the third.

Outside Roxanne's house, they chatted for a while, then Lottie looked at her watch saying, 'I had better get back, we have a full house this week and I must check we have enough of everything for breakfast. The punters love trying to catch us out. We had a couple of vegans staying last week and it was a regular nightmare. I am sure when they are at home they eat everything.'

Roxanne laughed. 'Good luck with that. See you around Lottie, bye.'

As Roxanne pottered about in her kitchen getting herself a toasted cheese sandwich she could not get rid of a feeling of foreboding concerning Aurora out of her head. I am just being silly, she thought, and decided to phone her in the morning to check all was well.

That night as Aurora was upstairs getting ready for bed she heard the noise of a small engine coming up the Creek. This was odd as boats were usually only around in daylight and it was now almost pitch black. Going to the window, she could see the beam of a flashlight guiding two men on to the Hard from a small boat that had just beached.

The figure that had remained in the boat looked up and saw Aurora standing outlined at the window and watching them. Shouting to the two men, he jumped out of the boat and then suddenly the clouds parted, and moonlight lit the scene. Aurora could see that in his other hand, he had a pistol and he started to run towards the house.

Then she heard it. The whoop---whoop---noise that she had heard before and an object flew through the air and hit the man in the neck. As he fell, the gun went off and one of the other men fell screaming to the ground while the remaining man stood frozen with fear before then running away up towards the road.

It only took Aurora a second to pick up the phone and dial emergency. 'Please come quickly, a man has been shot and another one is on the ground.' Then she gave her address. After describing that, she was looking out of her window at two men lying motionless outside on the ground. The operator advised her not to go out but to wait for the police and ambulance services to arrive. Before hanging up she heard the operator saying, 'Another incident at Hellham Creek, what on earth is going on?'

Within minutes, a police car and an ambulance were at the scene. It was like a rerun of the previous incident. Aurora put on her coat and went outside to join them.

Inspector Musgrave was bending down looking at the two men on the ground. 'I am afraid one of the men is dead from a gunshot wound and the other one, who is still holding a pistol, has similar marks on his neck to those that killed Mick Stein. Did you see what took place Mrs Graydon Boles?'

'Yes, I heard the noise of a motorboat when I was in my bedroom upstairs. As this is unusual at this time of night, I went to the window and saw the two men get out of the boat, then the man who was still in the boat saw me, and getting out he ran up towards the house waving a gun ...' Aurora paused for breath. How could she describe the odd noise and flying object again without sounding as if she was mad? 'A shot rang out as the man with the gun tripped and one of the other two men screamed and collapsed. The third man ran away up Creek Road.'

'See if you can find him, Jones, he can't have gone far.' The Inspector said, and the young officer set off swiftly on foot, his wavering torch lighting the darkness.

Inspector Musgrave bent down and was examining something on the ground. 'Well how about that. It is exactly the same wood dust that we found at the last incident. Forensics has still not identified that yet.'

The dead man and the badly injured man were loaded into the ambulance, which then drove off just as Jones returned with a terrified looking man who was talking excitedly in very bad broken English.

'He says he had paid a lot of money to the skipper of the boat to smuggle him and his brother to England from France. In other words, he is an illegal immigrant. The man who owned the boat had told them he had landed here many times before and that this was a nice quiet place where no one would notice.'

Well done Jones, put him in the car.' The Inspector was once again scooping up some wood dust from the ground and putting it into a plastic bag which he sealed and placed in his pocket. 'Can I come inside and take a statement from you Mrs Graydon-Boles, while it is fresh in your mind?'

'Of course, Inspector, follow me.'

They left several police officers taking flash photos of the bloodstains and indents in the stony surface where the men had fallen.

Aurora phoned Pru, 'Can you come and stay tonight please? There has been another incident and I can do with your company.'

'Incident' Pru queried, 'Not more bodies?' she did not expect Aurora's reply.

'Yes, I am afraid one man has been killed and another shot here tonight. It is unbelievable what is going on. I will fill you in when I see you.'

'On my way.' Pru replied.

After throwing some night things into a travel bag, she walked down the stairs into the studio of the converted, former grain store barn situated on Mariners Wharf that she shared with her partner Leo. They lived in the loft above the studio area. It had been designed by Leo and was modern and spacious and had featured in many trendy magazines,

Leo was a renowned artist and illustrator who had designed the covers for Aurora's books and that was how they had all met.

'Darling, Aurora has been on the phone. There has been more trouble at Tideways and apparently, one man has died, and another has been shot. I said I would go and lend moral support, as she does not want to be alone tonight. Is that ok with you?'

Leo stood by an easel unaware that paint was dripping from his brush as he digested this news.

'Good grief, what is going on? Of course, we must help. Do you want me to come as well?'

'No thanks darling, I will take the car and although it is only a short distance it will be safer than walking. I will phone you if anything else happens.'

She kissed him and getting into the car drove along the unlit road and was passed by two police cars heading out of the village towards Hellham Market. Arriving at Tideways, she parked and retrieved her bag from the boot.

'Oh Prue, am I glad to see you.' Aurora was already at the door looking pale and shaky. 'The police have just left, and I need a drink.'

In spite of herself, Pru laughed. 'I'm not surprised, make that two.'

Aurora led the way into the sitting room and surveyed the rows of bottles in the cocktail cabinet. 'What's it to be, gin, vodka or brandy, neat or a fancy mix?

'Vodka and something fruity, please.'

'How about a Cape Codder? I have some cranberry juice in the fridge.

'Lovely.' Prue said, settling herself in the large chintz covered sofa.

After going into the kitchen, Aurora returned with a clinking bucket of ice and a carton of cranberry juice. With an experienced flourish, she filled the two glasses and passed one to Pru. 'Bottoms up'. She said, and then told Pru of the night's events adding, 'The oddest thing was that when I saw that object flying through the air, just before it hit the man I swear I heard the strains of Waltzing Matilda again. I did not tell that to the police, as they would think I was mad. Also, as they carried the dying man into the ambulance he was saying Mat and then a sort of mumble. I think he heard it as well.'

When she finished Pru thought for a minute. 'You have recently been to Australia; do you think there is a connection there?'

Aurora got up from the sofa and then returned with a rather battered grey backpack and started feeling around the inside.

'When my cousin Tony took me on a trip up the coast to see the more remote places I took this with me. I think I removed all the contents when I came home.' Suddenly she stopped, and then as she removed her hand it contained a large flat pebble.

'Well, I'll be blowed. I forgot that was on there.' she passed it to Prue who turned it over in her hand. There were several weird marks and outlines of birds roughly carved into the surface.

Aurora leant forward saying, 'Those carved marks were made by an Aboriginal man I saw in a bank in this remote town up north. He said it was his lucky stone. He reeked of drink and was obviously an alcoholic. He was asking for whatever was in his bank account. The clerk said it was only a few cents and that until his next State payment went in he could not make a withdrawal. Even though he was dirty and smelt of drink, I liked his cheerful smile, so I gave him some dollar bills. He thanked me and said all he had was his lucky stone, which he insisted I took. I had forgotten all about it until now. Perhaps it is lucky; something has certainly saved me from disaster more than once in the last few days. However, I would rather things calmed down, it has been one darn thing after another.'

'Perhaps tonight is the last incident. What are your plans now?'

'Well, Henry is in the middle of an important case in court so he cannot come here. I will drive up to our house in London and stay until next week. I feel the need for a change of scene. A bit of retail therapy is what I need at the moment.'

'Good idea, I will keep you posted if anything happens this end.'

'Thanks darling, I 'm exhausted shall we turn in?' Aurora yawned, and after taking the two empty glasses into the kitchen, they went upstairs. Prue knew the house well and took her bag into the guest room with a roomy bathroom attached.

'Good night, sleep well.' She called shutting the bedroom door.

After a leisurely breakfast, Prue headed home to tell Leo the details of the latest weird happenings that had taken place at the Creek, while Aurora secured and locked Tideways and drove up to London. Their house near Regents Park was cool and tranquil when she opened the front door. The high ceilings and black and white marbled floors in the hall were so different from the cosy clutter of the house she had left earlier. This was spotless, and the polished surfaces gleamed, due to the very professional cleaners who came in three times a week. They were identical twin sisters who had come over from Poland to seek a new life. As no one could tell them apart, they both answered to the name Nikki which solved the problem.

Upstairs in the master bedroom, Aurora gazed out of the window at the leafy scene of that part of town life. The sound of passing cars replaced the earlier ones at Tideways of birds and water lapping on the muddy shore. Going over to her large mirrored wardrobe, she reacquainted herself with her town clothes. Smart suits, long evening dresses, short little black cocktail dresses and rows of shoes with high heels jostled for space. Smiling, she peeled off her jeans and bulky jumper and replaced them with a smart grey trouser suit, pink cashmere sweater, black Cuban heeled boots and a chunky silver necklace. Surveying her reflection in the mirror, she nodded in approval. My life is always one of two halves she thought and casually turned on the television that faced the bed.

A familiar face looked out at her. 'What the----?' She exclaimed, and sat down on the edge of the bed. It was a picture of Marc and a well-known South American model. At first, the name escaped her then she heard the newscaster say, 'Bonnie denies being romantically involved with Marc, the lead guitarist and singer with the rock group, The Black Snake Oilers, who have been on tour in her home country.' There followed library photos of Marc and Merle with their numerous children or appearing on the red carpet at music award nights.

Retrieving her cell phone from her handbag Aurora rang Merle. A strangled tearful voice answered.

'Merle are you all right?'

'No, they say Marc is carrying on with that Latin scrubber.'

'Now don't believe all you hear on TV. I am going to grab a taxi and I will be with you as fast as possible.'

With that, she phoned for a taxi and ran down the stairs and out of the house. The taxi arrived almost immediately, and she gave the address in Holland Park where Merle lived. Arriving there to find about half a dozen reporters and several TV crews already outside. Aurora put on her sunglasses, and after paying the taxi driver made a run for the front door ignoring the shouted questions. Merle must have been looking out for her as the door opened as she reached it. Inside she gazed at the sight of a dishevelled and tearful Merle.

'Now come on darling, this will not do, you have the children to think about; do not let them see you like this. Where are they by the way?'

'Upstairs in the nursery, Nanny is getting them tea.'

The house that Marc had bought once he was earning big money and when the children started arriving was large and on four floors. It also had a basement, which he had turned into a sound studio. Many of the group's hit songs had been written there. The top floor was given up completely to their growing brood. Comprising of a nursery, playroom, several bedrooms including one for Nanny and a galley kitchen where she made breakfast and afternoon tea. She had also looked after Aurora and Merle when they were small and was as Merle put it, 'a pearl beyond price'.

'Have you heard from Marc?' Aurora asked, settling herself on a high stool at the breakfast bar in the large kitchen, while Merle poured out a coffee from the never off coffee maker.

'Only a text saying it is all lies, and he will explain when he comes back at the weekend. They have their final gig tomorrow and then they fly home. Do you really think it is just this awful girl making it up?'

Aurora did not say that this was not the first rumour she had heard about Marc's wandering eye however, after a pause, while she drank some coffee giving her time to think she said,

'Well, it is a strange life, being away from home for months on end with girls lining up for any publicity to help their careers. Stories are bound to be easy columnist fodder. I think you should ignore whatever you hear and just wait until Marc is back and then ask him.'

Merle was already looking more like her old self. 'Yes, you are right, what a lovely big sister you are. Shall we do a bit of retail therapy while you are here? Just to take my mind off things.'

Aurora patted her arm, 'That's more like it. I have to meet Henry at his club shortly and then we are going to see that new musical that is opening today. Tomorrow I have an appointment in the morning with my publisher, but we could meet for lunch after that.'

'Great, I will meet you at Selfridges Roof Garden Restaurant at one o'clock and we will spend some of Marc's money. That will make me feel better.'

They both laughed and after calling a taxi, Aurora ran the gauntlet of the press once more and joined Henry at his club.

'Hello darling, what a day!' She said, after kissing him and then explained the details of the drama concerning Merle and Marc.

'Well, he wouldn't be the first rock star to succumb to these breathless beauties. However, if the jury is still out we will take him at his word.'

'Spoken like the barrister you are.' Aurora gazed at him fondly thinking that she was glad he wasn't in show business.

When Aurora arrived at the restaurant next day, Merle was already there. They were shown to a table and then ordered a seafood starter, pasta mains and finished up with a wonderful chocolate concoction.

'Now let's shop.' Merle was in mega purchasing mode and headed for the exotic lingerie department.

'Marc is in for the full boudoir treatment when he gets back.' She winked at Aurora and people turned to stare as she let out a peal of giggles, helped by the numerous glasses of wine she had just downed.

Aurora knew that this was a desperate attempt at bravado and took her arm as she swayed noticeably. Merle was as good as her word and the number of carrier bags grew as they whirled round the store. Eventually, they emerged outside, and Aurora hailed a taxi, which first dropped Merle off at her house before travelling on to deposit Aurora at hers. Stepping inside she welcomed its calm feel after the bizarre events that were Merle's world.

The next day the television news carried an item about the final concert that The Black Snake Oilers had just given in South America. It had taken place in a huge open-air venue that had been packed to capacity with ecstatic fans. True fans had a twisted black snake tattooed on their arm. Wimpy ones had bought a press on transfer depicting the snake that they wore with pride just the same.

The final song had been a surprise. A sweating Marc had struck up a rendition of Waltzing Matilda with the rest of the group picking up the melody after the first couple of bars but looking extremely puzzled as they played.

'Once a jolly swagman.' Marc sang, and a group of holidaying Australians joined in with gusto. However, most of the audience looked at each other quizzically after expecting the finale to be one of Marc's latest hits.

After the group ran for the exit, Steve their Manager hustled them into the waiting black limos and then drove straight to the airport to board a waiting private jet. No interviews were given and there was no mention made of Bonnie who had been shown cheering madly and with a smug look of triumph at the concert.

Merle phoned Aurora as soon as the news item had finished. 'Did you see him?' she asked dramatically, 'He did not look well and what was that nonsense about playing Waltzing Matilda? It did not make sense.'

Aurora was glad that Merle could not see her face that had drained of colour. It was a sign that did not bode well, and she had been here before.

'Are you still there?' Merle queried.

'Yes, I cannot think of a reason.' She lied.

'Well Marc and the boys should land in about twelve hour's-time, so I am going to the airport to meet them. I need to show that Bonnie and the world that Marc is my husband. I will take Star with me as she is old enough to cope with the situation.'

'I am not sure that is a good move. What does Nanny say?'

'I am Star's mother and if I say it is okay that is that.'

Aurora had the feeling that Merle was a bit tipsy.

'Fine. Henry and I are just about to go back to Tideways now, so best of luck and stay cool. Keep in touch, bye darling.'

As she put the receiver down, Aurora had a sense of foreboding and the feeling that this was not going to end well.

Back at Tideways all seemed calm and the sight of the Creek was as reassuring as ever. Aurora avoided looking at the Aboriginal stone that she had hidden in her desk drawer. The weather was glorious, so she and Henry took their Enterprise class sailing boat called Seasprite out for a sail down to where the Creek ran out between the sand hills before joining the sea. Tacking back enabled them to sail close to the marshes and see all the wading birds digging for food.

'Can this get any better?' Henry said leaning out to balance the boat in a stiffening breeze.

'Nope' Aurora replied, pulling in the sheet as they went about, 'and you have got rid of that town boy pallor.'

Henry laughed showing his recently whitened teeth. 'My God, he is handsome', Aurora thought.

After returning Seasprite on its trailer back to the boatyard, they tidied the back garden before collapsing onto the swing seat with thick ham sandwiches and big mugs of builder's strength tea..

The headlines on the evening television news were that Marc had collapsed on the plane and was now in a hospital back in London. A representative for the hospital said that Marc was in a coma and that his wife was at his bedside. Test were being carried out and a tropical infection was suspected. He was gravely ill but stable. None of the other members of the group had so far shown similar symptoms.

A shattered Aurora phoned Merle who tearfully said that there was nothing to do but wait and hope.

'Be strong and let me know if there is anything we can do.' Aurora said, thinking the curse goes on, but she did not confide in Henry about the stone. His practical training at the Bar will only ask 'where is the proof?'

Henry left early on Monday morning for another week of scheduled slog at the courts. Aurora then got ready for the fortnightly meeting of the writing group that today was to be at Rogers' house. Since his wife had left him, for whatever reason it was never discussed, he had lived alone in Spyglass Lodge situated at the beginning of Creek Road.

Arriving at the same time as Prue, Roger greeted them both warmly saying, 'Lovely to see you girls, a bit like the heavenly twins. That only leaves Roxanne still to come.'

Roxanne arrived out of breath as usual with wild hair like a stabbed mattress and scattering her typewritten sheets of paper all over the floor. Once she was settled peace returned. No one mentioned Merle, although everyone had seen the drama on the television and read about it in the Sunday papers. It was like the elephant in the room, but Aurora was relieved. As everyone else, she treasured these meetings as an escape into the world of fiction away from everyday problems.

First, they all read their stories and then Roger handed out slips of paper containing an exercise about how to develop a theme: historic, religious or mystical. Aurora finished first and gazed around the large room containing treasures from Roger's many postings around the world. Ships in bottles jostled for space on shelves with jade bookends and soapstone figures. Carved native shields hung with crossed spears and framed photos of Military types, unsmiling but exuding strength and power. She came back with a jump as Thursa entered to ask who would like tea or coffee. Thursa was a domestic treasure who came in twice a week to cook and clean. In between Roger was happy to exist on sandwiches or visits to the Curry House restaurant in Marsbury Magma. He had developed his taste for spicy food from his time in Sri Lanka.

They all read out their exercise contributions, followed by Roger setting the home story subject that was to be about a dog, any dog. His thinking was that he could then write a spy and defector story including a sniffer dog being brave and locating soldiers buried in bomb blast rubble.

Just as they were all packing their notebooks and pens away, Eric, looking worried and out of breath was ushered in by Thursa.

'Excuse me, but I had to come and warn you that Mu has just come back from her walk along the bank with Prince and said she saw this big snake curled up on the path.'

'Oh my God, is she all right?' Lottie was starting a full panic attack.

'Yes, she is fine, apparently Prince barked and jumped until the snake slithered down the bank. Mu described it as having tiger-like markings with yellowish sides and a flat head. I have never heard of any snake fitting that description that is in any of the British reptile books.'

'That sounds like the Tiger Snake found in Australia.' Aurora said before she could stop herself.

Prue knowing the significance of this whistled a 'Phew,' and grabbed Aurora's arm.

'This is getting beyond a joke.' Aurora whispered to Prue, then picking up her bag made a quick exit leaving the others discussing the fact that they had never seen any snakes near the Creek, let alone Australian ones.

As Aurora entered Tideways, the phone was ringing. Dropping her bag, she ran into the sitting room and picked up the receiver. It was Sergeant Jones.

Hello, Mrs Graydon-Bowles, this is just to let you know that the wood dust has been identified as the root of the black wattle tree found in Australia. Apparently, this is sometimes used to make boomerangs. It might explain what hit both Mick Stein and that people smuggling guy, also why we could not find the weapon that hit them both. An expert that we spoke to said that occasionally they can shatter on impact.'

'Thank you Sergeant, for letting me know. It is all a mystery, goodbye.'

Aurora stood by the phone thinking of her next move. Then she went to her desk drawer and picked up the stone that she now believed was trying to protect her. Outside she ran down to the water's edge and hurled the stone as far as she could into the Creek. It was high tide and the stone disappeared into the swirling water.

As she turned and started to walk back there was the noise of a stone hitting the ground behind her. She started to run up to her front door, heart pounding, while the noise of the stone followed her footsteps. When she entered the house, she slammed the door and leant against it breathing heavily. Then she felt the letterbox lift and the stone fell onto the doormat.

Refusing to look at it, she now knew what she must do; return it to the Aboriginal man who gave it to her. On the computer, she booked a flight to Australia in two day's-time, and emailed Tony to ask that he meet her at the Airport.

I will explain when I see you she typed. Then phoned Prue, hoping she was home from the meeting.

'Prue I am going to take that stone back to Australia.' She said when Prue answered. 'There have been so many strange and uncanny things going on since I returned. Can you keep an eye on the house for me please? I will most likely be back in just over a week.'

'Of course, don't worry about things here. Have a safe journey, bye for now.'

After the plane landed Tony met her at the terminal and whisked her back to his large bungalow that he had lived in alone since splitting with his partner. Aurora explained about the various disasters that had taken place and finished with the stone chasing her back to the house. He smiled at her, thinking how strained she looked.

'There are mystical things that we can never explain however, a tribal talisman should be here with its owner. We will go back to the bank where you saw this man and hope we can trace him.'

Next day they set off heading north, first making sure they had plenty of bottled water and a full tank of petrol. Passing the same type of road kill on the road, the remains of wallabies, emus and small animals too squashed to identify as Aurora had observed on her first journey. There were patches of burnt vegetation on the sides of the road bearing evidence of the long dry conditions in these parts.

At last, they reached the town where Aurora had seen the man. Going into the bank, she went up to the counter and recognised the same bank clerk sitting on the other side.

'Hello.' she said, 'I was here a few months ago and there was- how can I put it? A guy who was very much the worse for drink, trying to withdraw some cash. He did not have funds and I gave him some money. Do you know how I can contact him, please?'

The girl stared at her. 'Yes, I remember you, it was a very kind gesture. Unfortunately, the man you are referring to has died, it was only a matter of time.'

The girl saw Aurora's disappointed expression. 'His son has a shop that sells lovely Aboriginal paintings and craft objects. It's just down the street from here, you can't miss it.

I would try in there. I expect he can tell you what happened to his father, who went by the name of Berri, which is short for Berrigan, an Aboriginal name.'

Aurora thanked her, and they found the shop with no trouble. Inside it was a riot of colourful native Aboriginal art. The bold designs and patterns were unique. Behind the counter was a smiling young man.

'Can I help you?' He said.

'Yes please, I came here to find a man called Berri who I now have been told has passed away.'

The man nodded, 'He was my father and yes, I am afraid he had one drink too many. Of course, he knew what he was doing. His remains are up at our native burial ground. It is sacred to our family; I am going there with my brothers and sisters in a few days' time.'

Aurora felt in her bag and then held out the stone. 'He gave me this, I would like you to return it to his resting place when you go there, please.'

The man took it and gazed at it in recognition. 'I wondered where this had gone, Berri was never without it. If he gave it to you he must have meant it to protect you and bring you good luck.'

Aurora smiled, 'Well... it did protect me, and it certainly made life interesting as well. 'I will be happy that it is back with its owner.'

After buying a couple of tablecloths with amazing, striking designs, one for herself and one for Prue, she and Tony left the shop and booked into the only hotel in town.

Sitting outside in the late afternoon sun, having a long cool beer, Aurora looked at the world news on her mobile phone. There was a picture of Marc and the caption read

'Famous Rock star out of danger and recovering.' She showed it to Tony who said. 'There are some things that defy logic, I think this calls for a chaser.'

Two days later Aurora was on a plane heading home. As it climbed into the fabulous blue sky between heaven and earth, she shut her eyes. Then opened them again with a start.

'Did you just hear the sound of music, playing the song Waltzing Matilda?' She asked the woman sitting in the seat beside her.

'Well it is an Australian airline, so they may have played it however, no I didn't hear anything.

Aurora could feel her neighbour thinking, 'All the way to London next to this nutcase!' Was she imagining things or was the spirit of Berri still with her? Only time would tell.

The Red Queens

Ella gazed round and soaked up the ambiance of the typically French small run-down bar.

'How quaint.' She whispered to Jonny who was trying to order a coffee for her and a brandy for himself in his rusty schoolboy French.

Pierre the bar owner smiled, 'Do not worry Monsieur, I speak quite good English, we have many, what you call expats, living in this village.'

'Really, that is good news.' Ella chipped in, removing her large sunglasses and now seeing the man for the first time. Her glasses were for effect only and entering the bar from the bright sunlight outside had temporarily blinded her.

'For sure, they will sniff you out before long, you will be asked to a barbeque, so they can see if they want to mix with you.'

Jonny laughed more at the use of the racing driver speak than the thought of rubbing shoulders with the sort of people he had come here to escape.

'Who are the main hostesses here, the eager types?' Ella enquired as she patted Macron, her perfectly clipped large French poodle.

The Bar owner shrugged in a typically Gallic way. 'People refer to them as the Three Red Queens. They run the social life round here.'

Ella would have liked to hear more about the Queens however, Jonny was more interested in the upcoming Tour de France. The race was one of the reasons they had rented 'Les Arbres' for a year before making it their permanent home. Ella was hoping to write her first novel and felt the rustic area in the Midi Pyrenees would be ideal for a budding author.

After chatting about the race that passed through the village, the bar was getting busy so Pierre left them to attend to his customers. As Jonny, Ella and Macron left several people swivelled on their bar stools to watch them go. In a small community like this, newcomers were of intense interest. They did make a striking couple. Jonny, with his thick white hair and matching white moustache looked distinguished, while Ella was petite and stylish. Her light tan enhanced her short, off the face hairstyle.

It was not long before a neighbour called with a lemon drizzle cake. 'Hello, I'm Maureen, welcome to our village. I live in the mini chateau next to you.'

Ella laughed. 'Mini chateau, that sounds lovely.'

'Well it's too small to be a proper chateau but oversized for a normal house.'

Taking the cake from the pretty, smiling dark-haired woman. Ella said, 'Do come in, I'm starved of female company and there is something I want to ask you.'

When they were sitting in the cool main living room, each with a tall glass of lemonade and a slice of the drizzle cake, Maureen leaned forward, 'Ok so what do you want to know? I have lived here for nearly five years, so I am quite clued up about the social side.'

'Tell me about the Three Red Queens then I will know what to expect.'

'First there is Millicent, top Queen and a right snob. Always going on about her grand family and her education at a top boarding school. I don't think they taught manners at her school. If the conversation is not about her, she will always talk loudly to the person next to her to try to get the focus back on to herself.'

'Then there is Tilda, known as Tilly. She fires the guns that Millicent loads. She does not so much make a drama into a crisis as make everything into a drama. People are mystified when she apologises profusely for something that no one has even noticed. If you are wondering why they are called The Three Red Queens, it's because red is their colour of choice. Tilly has red everywhere in her house from her front door to her terrifying crimson bedroom. Millicent drives an ancient red Jaguar at breakneck speed, usually on the wrong side of the road.

That leaves Mina. Now she is the arch assassin. Never tries to be friendly, just sits and looks at everyone as if they are a bad smell. Mina has flame red hair, dyed of course. It argues with her ravaged complexion and the hair wins.'

'My goodness what about their other halves if they have them?'

'Lovely chaps, I would call them saints except that would give saints a bad name.'

'I'm dying to meet them all, I think I will take the bull by the horns and throw a barbeque myself. How about Saturday week? Will you come please?'

'I sure will, leave it to me to ask the whole group. If they all come, it should be about two dozen.' With that, Maureen kissed her on both cheeks French style and left an excited Ella dying to tell Jonny all about their illustrious neighbours.

It turned out that particular Saturday the Tour de France would pass by Les Arbres, so everyone would have a grandstand view. Jonny dug out all the chairs and tables from the garage and scrubbed the brick-built barbeque, while making sure he had enough charcoal and firelighters.

Maureen took Ella to the local shops where she advised on the best sausages and meats to buy; also, she said 'You must have sardines, halloumi cheese, tabbouleh and peppers for vegetarian kebabs.'

Really getting into the swing of things, she said, 'Now the best wine to get for a barbeque here is rose' and a Fruit Cup for the ones who have been warned to cut down on the stagger liquid by their Doctors.'

Luckily, on the day of the barbeque the weather was balmy. After a slight wrestle with the firelighters, Jonny got the barbeque going and soon the charcoal was glowing red-hot. Ella placed the salads, plate's cutlery and serviettes on a table on one side of the barbeque and the glasses, wine, beer and a big bowl of Fruit Cup plus ladle on another table the other side along with a lidded silver bucket containing ice cubes. Standing back proudly to admire their work she smiled at Jonny saying 'Let the fun begin.'

Everything was buzzing before Mina, the first of the Red Queens arrived with her much younger and hardly used husband Theo.

'Theo get me a drink.' She commanded, going over to an empty table, nodding imperiously to people as she passed. Mina had on a red mini dress, purchased from the trendy local boutique. The dress did nothing to hide her bony knees and scrawny legs. Once seated with her drink she sat alone under the striped umbrella and gazed critically at the house and garden from behind her gold rimmed spectacles attached to a gold chain. When not in use these spectacles dangled on her bosom, recently hoisted up by a very discreet plastic surgeon in Paris.

Tilly joined her. No one could have missed Tilly's entrance.

'Oh, do come on Rupert.' She shouted at the bent and puffing elderly man trailing behind her. 'Now go and get me a glass of strong Fruit cup and don't spill it.'

Rupert did as he was told and lurched gamely over the lawn, returning with a glass of Fruit Cup to which Ella had added a fair splash of brandy. Luckily, Maureen had warned her of Tilly's love of strong alcohol in her seemingly innocent tipple. Rupert had been a handsome matinee idol and his old-world charm was the only part of him that remained undimmed.

Mina put her spectacles back on and gazed at Tilly's attire.

'Why do you always have to copy me Tilly? You know I always wear red.'

'Oh, sweetie, red is my signature colour too. It is the dream theme for my house and all my clothes. If you have a go at me, I will have one of my turns. I feel quite faint already.'

'Do putt a sock in it Tilly, you're just a drama queen.' Then in an effort to change the subject, added, 'let's go and see what ghastly things these newcomers have on their barbeque.'

There was a queue at the barbeque where Jonny was enjoying his top chef role adding more food as it disappeared and turning things over as they browned. He had on a thick, dark blue apron with 'Jonny' written on it in big letters. It was a great way of introducing himself,

'What's it to be ladies?' Jonny said, tongs in hand when it was their turn. At that moment, a sausage exploded showering Tilly with a few spots of hot fat. She fell back against Mina who in turn fell against a young man waiting for seconds.

'Whoa,' he said, righting Mina. 'It's a bit early to be legless.'

'Cheek, this silly old woman fell against me.'

'Don't call me old, Mina. Everyone knows that you are at least ten years older than I am.'

Mina eyed the spots of fat on Tilly's jacket. 'Those spots won't come out. Bin it.' She smiled with satisfaction.

'I am really sorry.' Jonny said, however, I am sure a good dry cleaners can make that as good as new and I will pay.'

'It was new.' Moaned Tilly, pleased to be the centre of attention, 'I'm not hungry now, but I will try a couple of pieces of chicken and I think I can manage a sardine, a piece of halloumi cheese and a kebab.'

'Glad you're not hungry or there would be none left for the rest of us' Mina said scathingly eyeing Tilly's overflowing plate.'

'I see my other half is spreading her sweetness and light as usual.' Theo remarked to Patricia, a very pretty widow, as they sat on a swing seat away from the main crowd. He had been telling her the story of his life as he gazed into her very blue eyes. 'I told Mina I am utterly unreliable when we first met but somehow we finished up married.'

'Such a shame,' Patricia murmured letting the shoulder of her peasant blouse drop an inch. 'My husband died just after you tied the knot with Mina and I feel very lonely as I rattle around in my large chateau.'

Theo loved a sympathetic ear and moving a bit closer on the seat, resumed his tale. 'I am sick of red, red walls, red tiles, red bathrooms, red sheets, satin of course, red lights and an all red kitchen. I have red before my eyes. My optician has advised me to wear sunglasses indoors.'

'Ghastly.' Patricia let the blouse drop another inch, 'Do tell me more.'

There was a screech of brakes and a cloud of dust as a red Jaguar came to a sudden stop just before it hit a big ornamental plant holder. A tall female figure emerged from the driver's seat followed by a distinguished looking man who was shaking and pale.

'I wish you would let me drive Millicent, you will kill us both one day.'

Oh tosh, Pongo, don't you come over all colonial with me. If people will litter their drive with hideous objects what do you expect? This place needs tidying up.' She was dressed in a red caftan with a matching red jewelled turban and marched up to a startled Jonny hand outstretched. 'Hello, I'm Millicent.' She boomed.

Jonny did a double take. 'Good God,' he said before he could stop himself, 'I remember you. It's Silly Milly from the school we went to near The Elephant and Castle. You lived in Lewisham and your mother used to do charring for us when we lived in Blackheath.'

At that moment, the cyclists in the Tour de France whizzed past. No one paid any attention. This was far more exciting.

A Devilish Assignment

Lucifer was the fallen Angel who rebelled against God. He was in the offices of Original Sin when the slithering serpent passed a white envelope containing his next assignment to him. Today the serpent was in the form of a sylph like creature with long green hair and all over scales.

'Here is your next assignment on earth,' the creature hissed, 'now flap your wings, and be gone'.

Lucifer tore open the envelope as he made his way to the edge of hell and on to the launch pad. In large scrawl he read; Destination, Downbury Forest, objective, find the site of a yet undetected fatal accident and replace the victim. Your ultimate aim is to discover and eliminate the good Angel living in the vicinity.

This was exciting, he had been cooling his heels, or trying to for months in the baking heat of hell. Within seconds Earth came into view and he spotted the forest and the wrecked car that had rolled down the bank and was a tangled mess of metal jammed against a tree.

After landing, he pulled the dead driver out of what remained of the car. He had once been a nice-looking chap in his early forties, although now he was not a pretty sight. Lucifer quickly stripped the man's clothes from him and put them on, then he found a driving licence in the glove compartment of the wrecked car.

It stated that the driver had been Lance Handley, age forty-six. Address, 10 Oak Hill Road. Smearing some of the blood from the corpse over his face Lucifer lay on the ground and used his powers to photocopy the man's lesser injuries, features and memory on to himself. He then made the corpse disappear. He finished all this just in time as he could hear the sirens of police cars and an ambulance getting nearer.

'He'll live, the car must have skidded on that black ice, it's really bad tonight.' Lucifer could hear a voice say, although he kept his eyes closed. Then hands lifted him into the ambulance, doors slammed, and he was on his way to hospital. First part of the assignment completed.

A tearful person who turned out to be Jennifer, the wife of Lance Handley was at the hospital when the ambulance arrived. Lucifer kept his eyes closed but felt her tears fall on his face as she leant over him. 'Will he be ok?' she asked between sobs. Lucifer, who had an extremely well-developed sense of smell, caught a whiff of her expensive, strong perfume.

A strong male voice said. 'Nothing too bad, a few days here and your husband will be as good as new.'

What an idiot Lucifer thought and emitted a couple of groans just to let them know he was coming round.

'Oh, thank you Doctor, my darling is back with us.' A relieved and jubilant Jennifer gasped amid more tears.

After three days in the hospital, a private ambulance delivered him back to the large four-bedroom house in Oak Hill Road and the waiting Jennifer. Her devotion made Lucifer's toes curl, as devils do not enjoy devotion. However, it was necessary to play along as if he was a normal human being.

'You're so good to me.' he said when Jennifer arrived with a bowl of chicken soup and wobbly red jelly on a tray and put it on his bedside table. The minute she's gone, that's going down the toilet Lucifer thought. What horrible things these humans feed the sick. Devils do not need food, but he had to sometimes force food down to try to appear normal.

'Darling, when you're better can we go on a skiing holiday with the members of our tennis club. It's up in the Cairngorms and the snow is particularly thick this year. You've always been a brilliant skier and the exercise will be good for you.'

If I had really been injured, skiing would be the last thing I wanted to do. Lucifer thought however, he smiled and said, 'That sounds really great, you go ahead and make the arrangements.'

Jennifer clutched his hand, 'Oh thank you Lance darling. You'll meet a new club member called Dora who's coming with us, she's an absolute angel, helps everyone and is so kind.'

A month later, they were in a coach with assorted members of the tennis club and on their way up to Scotland. Jennifer introduced her new friend. 'Dora, meet my husband Lance, Lance this is Dora.'

As Lucifer shook the hand of a very pretty and cloyingly adorable, blonde girl, he was nearly overpowered by a sweet smell. He now knew who the object of his assignment was. It was Dora.

As the coach sped northwards, Dora moved up and down the aisle dispensing joy and homemade cupcakes to all and sundry. Congratulating people on their match scores or enquiring about their children. With every tinkly laugh, Lucifer felt his temperature rise. Looking out of the window at the snow-covered scenery, he knew that if he let his feelings of hate rise he would not be able to control steam coming out of his ears. This is what happens to devils when they get angry.

'Are you all right darling?' Jennifer asked with a worried look, 'we're nearly there'.

'Fine.', he replied, fixing her with a brave smile, 'just a little tired.'

Jennifer was getting on his nerves with her never-ending concern. However, Dora was his target and he was determined to complete his assignment at the first opportunity.

The hotel in Aviemore was near to the ski runs, and next morning the group caught the lift to the slopes. Lance had been a good skier, so Lucifer left Jennifer and continued up 'off piste' along with Dora. They left the others on the nursery slopes with the instructor.

After several initial runs, Lucifer spotted an unsuspecting Dora on the edge of a mountain ledge below him. Gathering speed, he swooped down and took off into the air clutching Dora. Her big feathery wings opened, twisting and turning in the air, they both hurtled down towards a deep ravine.

People on a viewing platform reported that they had seen a large white bird with enormous wings. It appeared to be in a desperate death struggle with a black winged creature that had a long arrow shaped tail and huge claws. As it grew dark, Jennifer in a fit of hysterics reported her husband and friend missing.

The mountain rescue team searched the area, but nothing was ever found. After a couple of days, the coach full of disgruntled would-be skiers and a red-eyed Jennifer, returned to Downbury with two empty seats

Wraiths Progress

Mr Jones was out in the fields. Dillys his daughter picked up the bucket containing the slops and went into the pigsty. The ramshackle outbuilding with its leaky roof had seen better days. Banging on the bucket and calling the name of Delilah, the enormous old sow who was queen of the sounder of swine, Dillys poured the slops into her side of the trough.

Delilah and the other pigs corralled in the small yard on the far side, hurled themselves at the food; grunting, snorting and they soon had their front legs in the trough, their snouts and soft ears covered in the revolting mess. The piglets, squashed and trampled on, squealed their protest.

A sudden gust of wind slammed the outside door and at the same time, a blast of cold air blew the dead leaves that lay scattered on the stone floor up into Dillys's face. Then she heard it, so faint it could have been way up in the distant mountains. 'Help me, save me', it repeated the desperate cry over and over. Dillys recognised the voice of her missing brother Billy. He had only been three years old when he disappeared six months ago. Her broken-hearted mother had taken to her bed and had hardly eaten since. Dillys opened the sty door and as the light flooded in the voice stopped. She leant against the wall and tried to stop shaking. Then she saw something on the floor that had not been there before, it was dirty and torn, but she knew it was the coat Billy had worn when he was last seen, playing with a ball outside the sty. What did it mean?

Later that morning she took a cup of tea upstairs to her mother's bedroom hoping that this time her mother would drink it. The doctor had told her that if Maud, her mother did not start to eat and drink soon he would not be able to keep her alive. All Maud did was lie with her face turned to the wall, her eyes shut.

As Dillys watched in fascinated horror, a grey and misty apparition rose from the bed and floated towards her. It was holding the hand of a little boy and they were both smiling as they passed her and disappeared through the wall. Running over to the bed, Dillys felt for a pulse in her mother's cold wrist. There was none. But as she lay there the corpse of Maud was smiling.

John the farm hand, later reported that Delilah had suddenly dropped dead, and that when clearing out the straw from her corner of the sty, he had found the lost ball belonging to Billy. The terrible truth then dawned on Mr Jones and Dillys.

'God rest his tiny soul', Mr Jones said as they made their way to the chapel for Maud's funeral.

The Great Wall and Bridge

It was the usual start to the afternoon Bridge session. The Chairman was on his feet announcing the name of a member who had fallen off the twig that week, and during the two minutes silence that followed, I racked my brain to put a face to the name.

Next, he read from a leaflet that described a Bridge holiday that included a trip to the Great Wall of China as well as Beijing and the Terracotta Warriors.

'How about it'? My husband and partner at the Bridge table muttered, as the Chairman rambled on.

'I'm game'. I replied and glanced over at my friend Joy and her husband who both nodded. So that was that, the trip was booked.

As usual, the afternoon was spoilt when, as East and West, we moved on to the table where Hamish sat. Being a physical wreck, Hamish had trouble moving but the more inactive and the more brain cells he lost, the more evil he became. His claims to fame, he told everyone, included being an atomic scientist, a professor at Harvard, an Olympic gold medal winner and a former Bridge partner to Omar Sharif. Ha, Bloody ha, to that.

Thinking I was a pushover, Hamish tried every cheating trick in the book, like claiming he had more winning tricks than he actually had and saying I had revoked. Instead of calling the Director, he would try to turn my cards over until they were so out of place that he hoped I would give in and let him win. Wrong, I would tell him he was not supposed to touch my cards; however, it spoilt the game, and mud for some people always sticks.

Unfortunately, Hamish also wanted his dose of culture and came on the tour to China with the group.

Leaving the coach at the start of the day at the Great Wall, we passed the many stalls selling souvenirs. The vociferous Chinese are determined to make you buy and after looking at their wares, a round jade paperweight, the size of a tennis ball, caught my eye. Carved in a ring around the outside, was the scene of the Great Wall. I haggled a bit, as we had been advised to do, then bought it.

Not wanting to carry the rather heavy object, I slipped it into my pocket. The Great Wall stretched impressively in front of us as far as the eye could see. It is the one thing that astronauts can recognise from space.

It was bitingly cold, though dry and clear. We started up the steps towards one of the beacon towers. The steps are difficult to negotiate, as they are deep and high. After going up a dozen, your legs ache and it's hard to get your breath. I was annoyed to see the one smoker in the group zoom past us on her way up. Arriving at the tower, she was enjoying her first cigarette of the day long before we joined her.

Hamish was making heavy going of it but eventually, he flung himself against the bit of wall where I was standing, away from the others, taking photos. As he stopped, he let out a sound like water going down a plughole, luckily, due to being out of breath I was spared his claims, that no doubt he had built the lot himself single-handed. He turned to look at me with those cold, fish eyes and I could not help myself, it was almost involuntary. As half of him was already hanging over the wall, I reached in my pocket and with my hand round the paperweight, leaned over and hit him hard on the back of his head. It looked as if I was trying to pull him back, but actually I was helping him on his way down into the chasm below.

The others ran up and viewed the mangled corpse lying among the rocks and weeds.

'You did try to save him, but there was nothing you could do.' They all said. 'You really are quite a heroine'.

My face was ashen however, that was due to the bitter cold wind that blew across the Wall, but inside I was warm with triumph.

Already the huge wings of the vultures were flapping above our heads. Their sharp eyes had spotted their next meal. We left Hamish to be buried, well what was left of him, in the shadow of the Great Wall.

That will be another two minutes silence when we get back to the Bridge Club.

The Seamen's Mission

It was a dark and stormy night as the old man shuffled up to the Seamen's Mission. Knocking on the heavy oak door that carried the marks of many sailors boots as they kicked out drunkenly when refused entry, the old man croaked 'Have you a bed for a tired and weary sailor?'

The kindly warden in charge peered through the grill then opened the creaking door. He was always wary about who was on the other side, as he had received many blows to the head from sailors who had downed too many shots of rum in the tavern next door.

The old sailor was not a pretty sight. Tall and bent with long matted hair, filthy clothes and a black patch over one eye. Inside the mission there was a motley bunch of sailors from the big ships that had berthed at the docks in the last few days. Some were old salts with many a tale to tell of voyages to foreign lands. Loudest of all was a young handsome man called Jack, regaling them with tales of his conquests of local women who hung around the docks at night. His favourite tales were of the butcher's wife, a buxom girl much younger than her husband, her infidelity was the subject of much gossip in the town. The old man after listening for a while lay on his narrow, hard bed and appeared to fall asleep.

The stories Jack told of his exploits with the butcher's wife got wilder with every shot of rum, while the other sailors' laughter became louder.

Next morning the old man was gone. Jack was discovered lying on his blood-soaked bed, his throat cut from ear to ear. Beside him was a matted wig, an eye patch and a very sharp butcher's knife.

The Shillelagh Murder

I could hear the dogs barking as they followed the trail of my scent. The beam of the police officers' torches were getting nearer to my hiding place in the clump of trees above the bay. It was inevitable that they would find me before long. How had it come to this?

We had lived on the island all our lives. I had bought the cottage and moved in when I had married over forty years ago. Becky had been pretty then, but the harsh living had taken its toll. The rosebud mouth was now a thin, hard line. The porcelain complexion lined and furrowed by the cold Irish winds that blew from the sea whatever the month or season.

A couple of months ago someone had broken into the boathouse that held all the gear that I used to run my salmon farming business. I used the boat to check the metal cages that held the young salmon and to feed them. The constant noise of the generator was annoying, but we got used to it, after all, I made a reasonable living from those fish.

There was another break in and more things were stolen. I did not tell Becky, knowing she would moan and blame me as usual. Amazing that... everything was my fault. However, I made the decision to lie in wait in the boathouse and catch those thieving robbers red handed.

I crouched behind the door with my Shillelagh at the ready. It had been passed down from father to son for many generations and the blackthorn wood was shiny and as hard as steel. It had fought many battles with drunken neighbours and even taken on rogues from the mainland.

There was no moon that night, as the cloud cover was low and the soft drizzle constant. The door creaked open and I could just make out a shadowy figure slowly entering. My shillelagh crashed down, and the figure crumpled, accompanied by the sound of china breaking. I switched on the light and a terrible sight met my gaze. It was Becky.

As I bent down I realised it was hopeless, she was dead. Becky had obviously realised where I was and had brought me a mug of tea. Everything swam before my eyes, I looked at the shillelagh still in my hand and the knob at the end was covered in blood and Becky's grey hair. Too late for remorse, self-preservation was what was needed, after all, it had been a genuine mistake but who would believe me.

I put Becky's body in the boat and rowed out to the furthest cage. First, I took off all her clothes, tied a weight to her lifeless form and tipped her over the side of the boat. Those fish would make short work of poor Becky.

When people asked where my wife was I said she had gone to see relatives but after a while rumours swirled round our small community. I had burnt Becky's clothes in the big kitchen range but detectives from the mainland crawled all over the cottage. Divers went down in the bay and I knew that eventually they would find Becky's remains in the furthest cage with the fish.

It was dark by then; the divers gave their report to the officer in charge and using my shillelagh to help me negotiate the rough terrain I reached the small copse. There were two options before me, prison or … no there was only one option. I climbed the tree, tied the rope to the highest branch, and formed a noose.

Scotch Mist

They arrived in the wild and beautiful Scottish countryside and looked for a place to spend the night. The last signpost they had passed, read *Inverheath Halt*.

'Let's try there,' Hazel said, 'I've had my fill of lovely scenery for today, what I need is a cup of tea and a shower.'

Dermot swung the steering wheel and reversed the car until they reached the one storey motel, built on the platform of what had once been a railway station.

A young woman showed them to their room and Hazel swooped on the tea making facilities. Soon they were drinking cups of hot tea and munching on the biscuits provided.

Holding her teacup in both hands to warm them, Hazel gazed out of the window. The view was stunning, a mossy bank dropped away to a Loch, the surface rippled in the breeze and a hovering osprey swooped down, emerging with a large struggling fish from the icy, grey water.

'Brilliant, an osprey is still quite a rare sight'. A thrilled Hazel remarked.

On the bedside table, a printed card stated, 'An evening meal can be arranged if required, Contact reception.'

Dermot who was not interested in wildlife, made for the door. 'I'll arrange for a meal for us tonight.' He said, leaving Hazel still gazing out of the window at the darkening scene.

After showering, they emerged to try to find the dining room. A smiling man; thirtyish, greeted them.

"Good evening, I am Tim Thompson the owner of the motel. Did you book to eat here tonight as I only had one request and they are already here?' He said looking puzzled.

'Yes, I told a lady at the desk. She just nodded, then turned and disappeared down the corridor. I thought perhaps she was going to tell someone in the kitchen.'

The colour drained from Tim's face. 'What did she look like, can you describe her?'

Dermot thought hard. 'That's not easy, it was quite dark, and her face was in shadow. She looked quite old fashioned and had on a shapeless dress and shawl. That's all I remember.'

Tim looked even more shaken. 'Please take a seat at the bar and I will get Marie, the girl you saw when you first arrived, to rustle you up an omelette and chips, will that be all right? I am so sorry about this and the drinks and food will be on the house.'

'What a rum place this is.' Hazel said as they found the small bar and hoisted themselves onto a couple of bar stools. Minutes later Tim arrived and going behind the bar asked. 'What can I get you?'

'A couple of gin and tonics, please' Dermot said, attacking the salted nuts on the counter while Hazel gazed round, taking in the row of mounted stags' heads and pictures of trains steaming along through purple heather-clad scenery.

Tim helped himself to a large glass of whiskey. After draining his drink, he leant on the bar and smiled. 'Shall I start at the beginning? I bought this place, unseen, about a year ago. I had worked in London in the money market but after my marriage fell apart, I chucked in my job and bought this place from a newspaper advertisement.'

When I arrived, for the first week, there was a thick mist that obscured the view. When the mist finally cleared, I saw the Loch for the first time. I couldn't believe how lovely it was. I knew nothing about running a place like this however, Marie has hotel experience and together we have made it a small haven for travellers like yourselves. It had at one time been a bustling station for the Spey Valley Railway line but closed several years ago.'

'I first saw the lady in a shawl one dark night when there was a gale and a door had blown open and was banging. As I went to shut it, a figure brushed past me and went outside. I now knew why I had been able to buy the motel for such a low price.'

Hazel eyes widened. 'You mean it was a ghost?'

Tim nodded as he refilled their three glasses, 'I made enquiries and I was told that in the 1930s, a woman who was waiting to get on the train fell on to the line just as it steamed in. She was killed outright and the rumours that swirled about were that her husband, who was the stationmaster, had pushed her in front of the train. He was having an affair with a lady who lived up the line. No one saw anything, so it was recorded as an accident. The ghost of the Stationmaster's wife haunts this place, although she hasn't done any harm, so far.'

Just then, Marie arrived to say their food was ready.

Getting up, Hazel smiled at Tim. 'Luckily I am not afraid of ghosts and your lovely hospitality will be the memory we will take away. In fact, I will give you a good write up on TripAdvisor.'

As they sat down in the dining room to their omelette and chips, Dermot whispered, 'It is wonderful what a couple of G and T's will do to make you brave.'

The next day they continued their holiday, visiting Glen Coe, Aviemore, where they went on the chairlift, the Fish Ladder at Pitlochry, finishing up in Edinburgh. It had all been excellent although the abiding memory for them both was of the haunted motel.

A couple of months later Hazel was listening to the radio when an item on the news made her stop in her tracks. It was about a tragic accident involving a mounted stag's head that had fallen off the wall of a Scottish motel fatally impaling a young girl called Marie Finley.

Miss Finley's grandmother, the newsreader continued, had been the lovechild of the married Stationmaster of the now closed Inverheath Halt Station and a young girl who lived up the line.

As Hazel turned off the radio, she felt sad for poor Marie, but wondered if the ghost at the haunted Scottish motel would now at last rest in peace.

Life's a Competition

'Was that the post?' Helena said to no one in particular, although Woofy her dog looked up in an interested sort of way as the two magazines and a letter dropped through the letterbox.

Helena had been halfway up the stairs at the time but executed a full turn, retracing her steps to pick up the items from where they had landed on the 'Welcome' doormat. The mat had been part of her prize of a full set of mats that she had won for completing a slogan for a firm selling household items.

She sat on the bottom step and read, through the plastic wrappings, that they were this month's editions of the two competition magazines to which she subscribed. The letter looked more interesting.

She raggedly tore the envelope open and read that she was one of the six winners for a weekend away on the Orient Express.

'How about that Woofy? That's something I have always wanted to do, travelling on a train from London to Paris, just as they did in the twenties. Such an elegant era.'

Woofy nudged her arm with a wet nose and looked up with his big brown eyes sensing a biscuit was in the offing. Absentmindedly Helena led the way to the kitchen and opened the door of a top cupboard in the run of brand-new units, part of her prize from a local installer. Her slogan was now on all their vans.

The cupboard, as well as being home for many tins of dog food also revealed dozens of packets of dog biscuits. The tins were minus their labels; these had been sent with her prize-winning entry. Woofy's new bed, blanket and a year's supply of dog biscuits had arrived only last week. Woofy loved that cupboard although he liked the new oven with its revolving spit even more. He and Smishy the cat would sit for hours in front of the oven's glass door watching a chicken go round and round on the spit. The oven had been the prize for a winning menu sent to a manufacturer of dubious crisps, the sort covered in a very salty, un-wholesome powder. Helena had sent the empty packets with her winning entry then given the crisps to a band of winos that congregated in the town centre. They were very pleased and said it complimented their raw alcoholic drinks a treat.

A cup of coffee was called for while Helena contemplated this latest bit of good news. She had started comping when Ralph, her husband had met with an accident when they were on holiday in Tenerife. Ralph, who was a complete duffer at sport, thought he would have a go at paragliding, having seen others easily flying high over the beach, Ralph thought he could manage this. He would take the official photos of his daredevil exploits back to show his co-workers at the Rates department at the local council. Especially Deirdre, the giggly blonde that all the guys were keen to impress.

The take-off went according to plan. However, a freak gust of violent wind had detached Ralph and his chute from the boat and sent him whirling away out to sea. A rescue boat had found him miles away with the chute wrapped around him. It had been on all the news programmes with Helena playing the bereaved wife.

Actually, Helena was tired of Ralph; he was the original grey man. The only times he tried to dig himself out of his boring rut it went wrong, like his paragliding adventure.

As she stirred her coffee, Helena thought of her first boyfriend Finn Finnegan. They had been at school together and had dated until Finn was seventeen. His father was a big noise in the army and when he was posted to Singapore the family had to move with him. Helena even now, could see Finn's dazzling blue eyes, hear his joyous laughter and remember his lovely, strong body. They had written long letters for a couple of years and then a shattering letter arrived to say Finn was engaged to a Eurasian beauty queen. In despair, Helena turned to Ralph who had been in hot pursuit of her ever since she had started temping at the council.

Life after Ralph was not exciting but different. She paid off the mortgage with the insurance money she received from the tour company and resisted the advice from friends to try on-line dating. Her time was filled with her hobby of entering competitions. The overflowing, object filled house bore testimony to her success.

Glancing down the list of the other five winners for the Orient Express competition, she felt her heart jump and race madly as she read a familiar name. Could it be? It was such an unusual name, after all these years was he once again unattached? She read it again several times aloud.

'Finn Finnegan. Finn Finnegan. Finn Finnegan.' Helena was suddenly full of hope. "I must find out, I will go on the Orient Express'. Mentally she made a list of what she would pack. Then panicking she ran to the mirror in the hall and examined her reflection. Did she look much different from her teenage self? Of course, she did. Perhaps some beauty treatments would help. Luckily, she had won the second prize in a competition for the sales launch of a chain of upmarket salons. Initially she had been a bit sniffy about the second prize that included a course of therapeutic massages, now it seemed heaven sent.

After booking an appointment, she rang the kennels. Woofy could hear dogs barking in the background as dates were made for his stay and knew what this meant. He hated the kennels and wished Helena would find a new man. Since Ralph had disappeared, Woofy's visits to the kennels had increased. He missed Ralph and their daily walks and often wondered where he had gone.

Susan's Pollution Issues

They sat in Susan's bedroom discussing the trendy musical event that was to take place that weekend.

'It's bound to rain, so we'll need our new gumboots.' Susan gazed lovingly at the brand-new pair of pink flower-strewn boots standing neatly by her wardrobe.

'And our denim shorts. I cut down my second oldest pair of jeans and fringed them last night.' Hazel, Susan's bestie was known for her ability to look right up to the minute despite her limited means. Pocket money did not go far if you were saving up for tickets to be at the latest boy band's open air concert. Razzle Dazzle Boy's concerts were definitely the place to be seen, even if as usual the venue next to the beach turned out to be muddy and wet.

'I'll wear my fringed poncho and take my sheer plastic mac as it's bound to rain, remember last year?' Susan got up and stared at her reflection in the mirror. 'I hope that hunky Josh and his pal are there again this year. My hair is much longer now, and I have lost a few pounds so maybe he will ask me out.'

'Didn't his nerdy friend Alex ask you to go on a date with him?'

'Fat chance with Josh around.' Susan pulled a face and flicked back her long blond hair. Just then, her mother called up the stairs.

'Girls, it's nine o'clock, time that Hazel went home. Don't forget you have volunteered to clean up some more of the stream tomorrow.'

'Just our luck that your mother works in the environmental department at the council.' Hazel said, putting on her denim jacket. 'But I suppose we must do our bit for the world.'

They both giggled and went down the stairs 'See you outside at nine thirty then. I'll wear my old boots for that, bye.' Susan shut the door thinking it was lucky her best friend lived next door.

The following day as they approached the small stream that ran through the village, armed with rubbish sacks, rubber gloves and wearing their old black gumboots, a Little Egret, with his long, raised head plumes, was standing in the shallow water surrounded by all sorts of plastic rubbish. Seeing them he stopped the sudden darting movements with his beak into the murky water and flapping his white wings, rose majestically into the air, showing his black legs and yellow feet.

'How about that?' Hazel, who was a keen birdwatcher gasped, 'I have never seen a Little Egret here before. Which proves that the time we spent last week clearing some of the rubbish away is appreciated.'

They set to work and by lunchtime, they had filled all the sacks with the rubbish that had found its way into the shallow stream. Thrown in by people who had eaten their pizza and drunk the accompanying Coke but were too lazy to find a rubbish bin.

'Where were they dragged up?' Hazel asked the overhanging trees, 'one day they will drown in rubbish and serve them right.'

Susan nodded and clambered up the bank. 'Gosh, I'm wet and hungry, just time to eat, have a shower and get glammed up for tonight.' With that, the two girls trudged off back to their homes.

The concert was wonderful. Susan jumped up and down to the music, the fringe on her poncho dancing in time to the beat. As the band took their bow to wild applause Josh and Alex saw them in the crowd and came over.

'Hi girls, Fancy a stroll on the beach?'

'Great!'

Susan could hardly contain her excitement. They chatted on about what they had done during the last year. Alex and Josh had gone to uni, although Josh had dropped out after a term.

'Boring, they didn't help me enough and I felt my talent wasn't encouraged.' Josh took a swig from the bottle he was carrying.

Alex winked at Susan. 'His talent was in ducking out of work and finding the nearest bar.'

Susan looked up at Alex. He had grown about six inches in the last year and had obviously been working out at the gym. Josh finished his drink and threw the empty bottle into the sea.

'That will most likely finish up thousands of miles away, perhaps by a coral reef. Don't you care about polluting the planet and killing wildlife?' Susan fixed him with a cold stare and wondered why she had thought him attractive.

Josh shrugged, 'Not my problem.'

Alex was already up to his ankles in the sea and after retrieving, the bottle had put it in a rubbish bin.

Thanks,' Susan smiled up at him, 'Do you remember you asked me for a date last year?'

Alex went a bit pink, but he smiled down at her. His green eyes warm behind his glasses.

'Well, a year is a long time,' they both laughed, and his hand found hers.

Seven Days Away

Mia and her best friend Lorraine have booked a week's holiday on the Greek island of Corfu.

They both work in the local branch of McDonalds in a town in Kent. Like a lot of young girls today, they are tall, slim, curvy and blond. Their interests are not what one would call of an intellectual persuasion.

They love going to clubs and attending raves and festivals that feature headline musical groups.

Mia has several younger brothers. Her mother has never thought it necessary to be married and her boast is that she is her daughter's best friend.   Mia thinks this is embarrassing as her only best friend or bestie is Lorraine. Her mother, Shiraz, takes to Social Media once a month to heap scorn on the fathers of her brood for not coming up with their maintenance payments. However, this does not stop her trips to the gym or to the hairdressers for a bleach job and hair extensions.

Mia and Lorraine have bought an entire holiday wardrobe from Primark, paid for with tips from work and birthday money. These items are packed into the shiny plastic wheelie cases that they have bought from the local supermarket. Their cases also contain their makeup and tubes of sunscreen. Mia's case is pink, and Lorraine's is green, both have flower designs all over them.

The night before the big day, they have both sprayed each other liberally with fake tan. Unfortunately, the only ones in the reduced range they bought were made for 'people of colour' so they were at least ten shades darker than their skin tone.

Day one. We arrived at Stansted Airport in a white van owned by Lorraine's father and wheeled our cases through the revolving doors. Queueing up to go through Security, we saw the sign that said you must not take food beyond this point. Shiraz had made us each a doorstep jam sandwich, so we ate them quickly and as they had stuck in our throats, we washed them down with the Cola that we had just bought. We also had to abandon the rest of that. Very excited getting on the plane but we could not sit together as our numbers were miles apart. I had a horrible, grizzly child behind me who kicked the back of my seat. I turned around and pulled a terrible face at him. That made him cry for the rest of the journey. His Mum was not pleased. Getting off the plane the heat hit us like a blast from an oven. Cool, if you know what I mean.   Arrived in a coach at the resort and got off at the Hotel Splendide, which is huge. The beach is in front of the hotel and only separated from it by the motorway. Our room is at the back but has a balcony. The lift is not working so we have to climb the six flights of stairs. Not good if you are a geriatric, but ok for us as we expect to eat and drink a lot as the hotel is 'all in'.

Day 2. Swam in the pool and found a couple of sun loungers that were not broken, so caught some rays. Chatted up by the waiters, the pool attendant and the Entertainments Manager who made us join in his poolside games. We threw him in the pool as he was a bit everywhere with his hands and we only had on our bikinis.

Day 3. Went to the beach and had a ride on the yellow banana that has eight seats and is towed by a speedboat. Met two boys from Scotland and promised to meet them in the town that night. We think that is the arrangement, but we could not understand a word that they said. They did not turn up, so we may have got the meeting place wrong. Had some laughs however, with some local boys.

Day 4. We won the Karaoke competition singing 'Working nine to five' and the prize was a date with the hotel D J who is also the Entertainments Manager with the wandering hands. We won't bother with that.

Day 5. Disaster as our fake tans are flaking off and we look like blooming hyenas. We decided to keep our jeans on, which made us very hot as we walked along the edge of the beach. We found a couple of boys hiding in the bushes. They said not to tell anyone that they were there. They were in an 18~30 group but they couldn't take any more of the alcohol or wild games. We took them back to our room and showed them our patchy tans. That made them feel a lot better.

Day 6. Met the two boys escaping from the 18-~ 30 group after lunch and went on the Pirate Galleon with them. They are good swimmers and did the swinging out and then dropping into the sea bit. We climbed down the ladder and joined them. The water was lovely. They live in Brighton and have asked us down for a visit. We said yes. Packing tonight. Sad.

Day 7 In the coach on the way to the airport. That's our holiday over for another year. We took loads of selfies on our mobile phones to show off a bit when we get home. Roll on next year.

The Dinner Party

'Apologies madame for taking up three chairs, but my dress is a trifle grand. I introduced this type of fashion to the French. Before me they had no idea of style.'

I gaze at this lovely lady in an impressive blue dress of finest silk. It has an enormous skirt of many layers; hence she is sitting with an empty chair either side of her, one of which is between us as we sit at a long table flanked by many famous people. I cannot take my eyes off her tight bodice, with its gold embroidery and lace from which her ample curves fight to escape.

'Tell me my dear why are you here are you famous, a queen perhaps?'

I laugh at the idea. 'No, your Royal Highness, I won a competition in a magazine about history to attend this banquet and requested that I be seated next to you, or as it turns out nearly next to you.'

'How very kind, I have not been out with my head on since 1793 and it is extremely satisfying. Oh la la, food.' She clapped her tiny hands with their many diamond rings. 'I have not eaten anything since that ghastly man cut off, not only my lovely hair, but also my head. His name was Henri Sanson and he became famous for his butchery, however not as famous as I am, even now.'

The waiters placed a prawn and lobster cocktail in front of us. Marie Antoinette, one-time Queen of France recoiled in horror.

'What is this abomination? I was hoping for larks' tongues or a delicate consommé.'

'This is quite a traditional starter today and most people find it enjoyable.'

The Queen fluttered her fan then picking up a fork tried a tiny piece of lobster. As she chewed delicately, her expression was one of bliss.

'The sauce is piquant, and this fish thing has a fine texture and taste. I like it.'

With that, she finished her prawn and lobster cocktail then took a sip from one of the three wine glasses in front of her.

'This is a French white wine, are they trying to insult me. I like German or Austrian wine, French is too thin. I was born in Austria and my father was the Holy Roman Emperor, Francis the first, and my mother the Habsburg Empress, Maria Theresa, therefore I was brought up on wine from that region.'

'These days, Your Majesty, we drink wine from places like Australia and South Africa.'

The Queen turned her wonderful long lashed eyes on me. 'I have not heard of those countries, but I am told that there is a town called Marietta in Ohio in the American colonies that is named after me. I like to think that at least I am remembered. She leant over and touched my arm. 'As I am only here because you asked me. You may call me Marie Antoinette and ask me anything you like.'

At that moment, the waiters cleared the empty plates, replacing them with plates of Sirloin steaks served with a rich jus. Dishes of steaming vegetables followed and were placed in the centre of the table.

The Queen viewed her plate with incredulity. 'You do not eat much today,' she said, 'this would have been the amount a peasant would eat. When I was at Versailles we had many courses of elaborate food that took an army of chef's days to prepare.'

I looked at her tiny waist and wondered how she had kept it that size then gazed at her elaborate hairstyle. 'Your Majesty, I read that your hairdresser Henri-Autie, sometimes designed styles that rose to nearly four feet in height. That these involved feathers, jewels and even a model of a French warship. How did you manage to keep your head up?'

Marie Antoinette smiled as she recalled those days. 'Yes, it was hard, however, we Royals were tough. At that time, everyone loved me, and I wanted to put on a good show.'

'I read that you were the youngest of fifteen children born to your parents and that you were married at fourteen, that seems incredibly young.'

'Yes, in order to seal an alliance between Austria and France, a marriage between the fifteen-year-old heir apparent to the French throne, the Dauphin, Louis-August, and I was arranged. We were too young to realise what we were supposed to do, and I did not have the first of our four children for seven years after our marriage.'

Our conversation moved seamlessly from one topic to another, covering many aspects of her life as Queen, after her husband became King Louis XV1.

She picked delicately at her food remarking, 'The British cuisine has improved remarkably since the period when King George the third was on your throne. If I was alive today I would consider a state visit.'

As the wine flowed and an individual Pavlova topped with strawberries was served to every guest, I asked about the quote that everyone knows.

'Your Majesty did you really say, "Let them eat cake"?'

Marie Antoinette, Queen of France was savouring her Pavlova with a look of dreamy delight. 'Wonderful,' she murmured, 'it makes me forget everything.'

I woke up just as the hire car pulled up outside the plush London hotel. As the driver opened the car door and helped me on to the red carpet, a person who I assumed was an actor came forward to greet me.

'Allo Mademoiselle. Je suis Marie Antoinette' she said in a terrible attempt at a French accent. Like hell you are I thought, but smiled at her as we walked through the revolving doors into the dazzling reception area.

She was wearing a rather grubby stage costume vaguely of the era of the French Revolution. Accentuating her badly applied makeup were several black beauty spots. On her head was an enormous nylon wig that was tilting to one side.

A waiter came forward with a tray of Champagne. We both gratefully took a glass.

'Bottoms up' the stage Marie Antoinette said, then remembering her script added, 'I mean, a votre santé.'

I sipped the chilled, and very good Champagne, thinking perhaps the food would be inspired. I stared round at the other prize-winners standing with their chosen dinner guests. A large man waving a cigar who was proclaiming in a loud voice, I assumed was an actor playing Winston Churchill. A disabled man with a missing arm in old-fashioned navel uniform and wearing an eyepatch fitted the description of Admiral Lord Nelson. Several whiskered men defeated me but were most likely famous writers or scientist from long ago. A couple of buxom actors could have been movie star lookalikes for Marilyn or Lana. I knew my Marie Antoinette did not have a clue who they were meant to be.

At last, dinner was announced, and we trooped in to take our place at the beautifully laid table under twinkling crystal chandeliers. The food was excellent however, I still cancelled my subscription to the glossy history magazine when I got home. One can never recreate the past.

The Princess Bible

Pippa shook her head vigorously.

'I think you are most unkind to call me 'A Princess', I just like nice things and luckily I get them. I think you're jealous because people do spoil me.'

'No, you are lazy and vain.' Lucie slammed the front door of Pippa's Essex semi, that looked exactly like every other house in the row, then stomped up to her five-year-old Minivan that was in need of a paint job on the left-hand bumper where someone had backed into it while it was parked.

Driving along to deliver the homemade birthday cake that was in the shape of a spaceship, Lucie fumed at the unfairness of life.

Why did she have to graft making these hateful cakes while her sister floated around as people queued up to offer her help and everything she wanted, even before she knew she wanted it?

Back at the semi, Pippa clutched her tiny fluffy dog to her fluffy low-cut jumper.

'Come on Miss Pink it's your turn to be beautified today'.

Miss Pink reached up and licked Pippa's peach bloom cheek, eliciting a hasty shudder as Pippa wiped her cheek with the back of her hand.

'No Miss Pink, not mummy's face. Now we must hurry as the girls from Maisie's Mops Ltd will be here soon.'

The two cleaners were essential to the smooth running of the house. They tidied, changed the beds, loaded or emptied the dishwasher and either took out or retrieved the bins. Princesses did not do bins. Just imagine if a rogue photographer from a trendy magazine happened to be hiding in the bushes. The shame of it, Pippa the Essex 'it' girl snapped with her rubbish bin! Even the dog shuddered at the thought.

Hastily throwing on an up to the minute fake fur jacket Pippa opened a drawer, threw Dustin's framed photograph inside, and slammed it shut. Dustin was amusing but she had her sights set on Hugo, the recently divorced multi-millionaire who had, so rumour had it, just moved into the area. Her spies, Timo and Greg had promised to track him down but so far had failed.

With Miss Pink safely in her small baby seat, Pippa drove first to the doggy beauty parlour, leaving Miss Pink with the three cooing assistants she gave instructions to renew the bright pink hue to her white fur. Then after forcing a tear as she left, drove to the nearby wine bar. This was where the cast of their hit TV reality show met to exchange gossip and flirt outrageously.

Entering the smoky glass and shining chrome interior and exchanging air kisses with everyone, Pippa sat on one of the high bar stools.

'Well what's new?

'The show has been cancelled,' Timo announced dramatically, 'we can't believe they would do this to us.' His face was ashen beneath the layers of fake tan.

'What? Why?' screamed Pippa, 'We are a huge success.'

'You mean we were, the studio phoned to say the viewing figures have plummeted. We are yesterday's news now.'

There was a sobbing group hug. Other customers let their wine trickle down their chins as they observed this tribal display of sorrow.

'Hells bells has the Pope died or the TV presenter of the local news programme actually retired her old dresses and bought new ones.' one wag observed. 'It's as if a global disaster has hit.'

'What will we do?' wailed Trudy.

'I can't do nine to five.' Timo grimaced at the thought.

'I suppose we can always do one of those reality shows where they abandon you on a desert island.' Greg, who was not renowned for his brainpower observed.

'Oh, do shut up,' Snooks gave him a withering look; 'I am not eating insects or fish eyes for any old TV programme.' Changing her mind about ordering a prawn roll.

'I suppose I could write a story for children about Miss Pink.' Pippa said, 'Even comedians and actors are doing it these days.'

'Oh, come off it, you couldn't write a laundry list unless you had a ghost writer do it for you.' The waspish Trudy tittered.

Pippa jumped off her high bar stool managing to knock Trudy's wine into her lap.

'Oops sorry. I must fetch Miss Pink. Boys do let me know if you track down the elusive Hugo, he is my only hope.'

'He wouldn't bother with an old has been like you.' Trudy muttered under her breath.

Pippa flounced out of the wine bar and drove along in a panicking state; this should not happen to a girl like her.

Arriving at the doggy beauty parlour, she picked up the now bright pink dog and passed over her credit card.

The owner standing at the till gave her a sharp look.

'It has been refused, I will take cash darling.'

'Pippa looked in her purse. Luckily, she could just scrape up the amount displayed. Was this the sign of things to come?

'I'll phone the card company and sort this out, I have lots of credit left.' She lied, thinking, I should have read those last warning letters and not stuffed them in a drawer, which was her method of filing.

Meanwhile Lucie found the address to deliver the birthday cake. It was in the most prestigious road in the area. The sold sign was still outside meaning that the owner had only recently moved in.

As she knocked on the front door, it swung open. The noise of children shouting inside was deafening.

'Is anyone home?' she called out and a tall tousled man with a distraught expression emerged into the hall.

'I have a birthday cake for someone called Richard' she tried to hand it over, but the man was too distracted to take it from her.

'Can you put it in the kitchen?' He said and rushed back in the direction of the noise.

After finding the kitchen and noting how fabulous it was, Lucie went in search of the man in the hope of payment. She found him in a vast empty room where about ten boys were shouting and jumping off large packing cases.

'Without thinking she shouted 'Quiet,' at the top of her voice.

There was instant silence.

'Sorry,' she said to the man, 'I shouldn't have done that. I am a Scout leader and I used to be a teaching assistant, old habits die hard.'

I'm glad you did, my Au Pair and housekeeper have just done a runner and I didn't have time to cancel Richards's party. I don't know what to do.'

Lucie thought for a minute then an idea struck her.

'If you like I'll phone a friend who runs a fast food restaurant and they do children's parties. They have entertainers and clowns who keep the children amused.'

'The man nodded, 'Oh please do.' he said, 'by the way my name is Hugo, I employ thousands of people and at work I am completely on top of things however, with children I am out of my depth.'

Well of course you can't sack them, Lucie thought, getting out her phone and ringing her friend Freddie.

'He can fit us in and I told him we have the cake.' Lucie relayed to a now smiling Hugo. Six children were loaded into Lucie's Minivan and the rest into Hugo's big Land Rover.

As the clown did his routine and the children tucked into the modern equivalent of a medieval feast, Hugo turned his green eyes on Lucie.

'You're just what I need. Since my divorce, I haven't been able to cope with the children and all the domestic side of things. Will you come and work for me? I'll pay you a top salary, and when we go to one of my houses abroad I would like you to come with us.'

Lucie laughed. 'And you don't even know my name. But the answer is yes.'

'Hugo smiled back; his green eyes had lost their distraught look. 'That turned out to be a lucky birthday cake.' he said.

The Little Black Dress

Heather arrived at the airport and got out of the car.

'I'm afraid it says no waiting; do you want me to park the car and see you to the check in?' Paul said, looking as if he wanted to make a quick exit.

'No, I am ok from here.' Heather took her small suitcase from the back seat and without a backward look went in through the revolving doors. The airport was quite busy, but her flight to New York was already checking in and she joined the queue. When it came to her turn to weigh her suitcase the attendant raised her eyebrows.

'Not much in there.'

'I always travel light.' Heather replied, thinking but never this light. The only thing inside her case was a little black dress.

As the plane took off and the green fields of England stretched below she leant back in her seat and closed her eyes. Was she excited or sad? Probably both.

It all started a month ago, Heather had returned home after her shift in the town's only department store. Paul worked from home as a freelance IT consultant. Their next-door neighbours, Joan and her husband Phillip were sitting on the sofa. Nothing unusual there as they often went out as a foursome, what was unusual was the tense atmosphere, Joan's tearstained face and Phillip's stony look.

Phillip spoke first, 'Your husband and my wife have been having an affair while we are both out earning a living.' he said tersely. 'I'm moving out and I thought I should tell you before I went. I'll sue for divorce and drag them through the courts. What do you think you will do?'

Heather sat down heavily in an armchair. Everything swam before her eyes while she thought about this startling news and their life together. She had been married for fifteen years and they had jogged along quite happily. It had been a toss-up between marrying Paul and going with her first sweetheart Gavin to Australia. At her young age, Australia had been a step too far, and her widowed mother had cried and said it would be heartless to leave her so soon after Heather's father had died of a sudden heart attack.

On her eighteenth birthday Gavin had given her a little black dress saying, 'Now you are all grown up you can wear this and I will take you to the most sophisticated restaurant in London'.

Heather would always remember that night. As they were escorted to their table by the maitre 'd, all eyes had swivelled as she walked past the other diners, wearing the short, black dress. She had been very slim and the low-cut neckline emphasised her eye-catching curves.

The meal had been great, especially when the waiter had cooked crepe suzettes by their table and served them straight from his flaming trolley on wheels.

'I will always remember this night and how you look in that dress.' Gavin had said as he smiled, and his soft brown eyes said the rest.

'Tea or coffee?' the airhostess said, bringing Heather back to reality with a jolt.

'A gin and tonic please.' she said, thinking that will be my last drink until I can fit into that dress again.

Her plan was to explore New York then fly to San Francisco, hire a car and drive down to Los Angeles. Next, fly to Hong Kong then to New Zealand and finish up in Perth, Australia.

What had started her plan was a Christmas message on her mobile phone from Gavin. He said that another former school friend of theirs had visited him and passed on her details. Gavin had described how he had a nice house in Freemantle, that he had never married, but described how various girls had flitted in and out of his life over the years. 'Why don't you and Paul come out for a holiday?' The message ended.

Heather had not told Paul or replied to Gavin however, she would send a reply when she could get into that little black dress. It would mean losing a couple of dress sizes, but I will do it she promised herself.

Her mother had remarried and no longer needed her around. Paul had not wanted children, so she had no family to worry about. Unbeknown to Paul she had saved up a small nest egg or running away money over the years. I will use that and do my trip on the cheap, she told herself. I'll be like a student on a gap year.

In New York no one took notice of the thirtyish girl in jeans, a black tee shirt and trainers walking round museums and art galleries, she looked like any other tourist. She found a cheap hotel just off Times Square and every morning visited the diner beside it for coffee and breakfast before setting out. All the things she had read about were being ticked off her bucket list. China Town, Central Park, the Statue of Liberty, a couple of skyscrapers and several Broadway shows. Next, she flew to San Francisco, hired a car and after visiting the famous sights around there, drove to Los Angeles stopping off in Hollywood.

A visit to Grauman's Chinese Theatre where famous film stars had left their hand or footprints in the sidewalk was a highlight. Heather put her foot in the imprint left by Marilyn Monroe's tiny foot and found hers by comparison was excessively big.

Then throwing her case in the rubbish bin at the Airport, after transferring the little black dress into her backpack, she caught a plane to Hong Kong. In Kowloon where she had found a cheap but clean hotel, she could easily catch the ferry. The sight of the main island at night with its myriad of twinkling lights shining from the many tall buildings was fabulous. At the bustling markets, she bought some new Tee shirts, jeans, trainers and underwear, throwing her well-worn ones away, while stowing some extra ones in her backpack with the dress.

Then on to Christchurch in New Zealand. She had been away for six months and was getting tired of the nomadic life, after taking in the sights she bought a plane ticket to Perth and sent a text to Gavin, it read: Arriving tomorrow at Perth Airport, 2pm. Will you meet me? Heather.

Just before the seatbelt sign went on she went to the aeroplane's toilet and with some difficulty changed into the little black dress. Would it fit? It did and with room to spare.

At the meeting area, she gazed round eagerly. And there he was, looking just the same but with a deep tan. The soft brown eyes smiled their happiness

'Hello Heather', he said, 'You haven't changed a bit and you still have that little black dress.'

Authors Revenge

It was the evening of the Writers' Club's weekly Thursday meeting.

Marcia opened proceedings with apologies for absence from Deidre and Martha, who were apparently sunning their bodies in various different hot spots.

'All right for some,' muttered Joyce, gazing at her pale, wobbly bingo wings.

This elicited a crushing look from Marcia while June sitting next to her stifled a giggle.

First, they all read their homework stories. The standard was first class as they had notched up a high standard of writing over the years and they had all published several novels.

Each had their own style of writing and could tackle any subject from romance to murder. Joyce had just had her latest novel, a thick tome of romance published. It laid in front of her on the table, it's pretty cover on display.

At half time as they drank their tea or coffee and munched on Marcia's, drizzle cake, Betty raised the question of promotion and if the one and only department store in the town would be stocking the book.

'Old Mr Fred Hogbin is so lovely and sits in his office and chats for hours about any new book I take in.' 'He has a special area just for local authors.' Alice said, picking up Joyce's book and flicking through the pages.

Joyce shook her head angrily.

'Not anymore, Fred Hogbin has retired and a new upstart called Damian Billinghurst, has been headhunted from London, and believe me he is an entirely different kettle of fish. When I took my new book in and asked to see the book buyer, that spotty girl on the counter said, 'you'll be lucky, he only sees authors by appointment after you have sent in an email requesting an audience.' Joyce continued leaning forward and jabbing her pen in the air. 'This depends on you answering about a hundred details, designed to rule you out. I think he only wants to deal with 'bestselling' authors, so he can get them to do book signings.'

'What a cheek'. Betty exploded, 'he needs taking down a peg or two.'

After that, the rest of the meeting degenerated into a rant about Damian and how he had ruined their chances of getting recognition for all their work. Marcia cleared the cups away and produced a bottle of fine sherry. As she explained, this was an emergency and direct action was called for.

'This Damian chap is a health fanatic, the sort you see buying health supplements but never looks healthy. He goes for a run every night down Lime Kiln Way. I know because he runs past my house in his 'oh so correct- running gear.'

Joyce held her glass out for a top up. They all did the same.

Ten minutes later someone said, 'Let's go and tell him what we think of him and his uppity ways.'

'I'll drive', offered Marcia, 'I've been so busy filling up your glasses I've only had one glass of sherry. Oh damn, Tom next door always leaves his van on my drive as his wife is a midwife and goes in and out, so he is blocking my garage.'

'Can't we take the van, I saw it had seats in it when I came in? Joyce was always a problem solver.

'Of course, he always leaves the keys in it as sometimes I have to move it.'

Marcia was already out of the front door and climbing into the driving seat of the white van. The others clambered in behind her. They drove along in the direction of Lime Kiln Way.

As they reached Ferry Lane, someone shouted,

'There he is.'

A lone jogger came into view illuminated in the headlights as Marcia slowed down. Then Joyce opened the door and several hands grabbed the surprised man and pulled him on to the floor among the sensible shoe clad feet.

'What the....' Damian puffed as a torrent of blows from books and shoes rained down on his head accompanied by unprintable language.

'Teach you to belittle us you worm.' Someone shouted, then after several minutes, the door opened, and he was pushed out.

Marcia peering in the driving mirror saw a car behind pull up and someone get out.

'Hell, someone has found him. Let's scarper.' She said.

They screeched off and soon were back at her house. The van was on the drive exactly as it had been twenty minutes before.

After receiving the emergency mobile phone call, the police and ambulance arrived and found a dazed man in jogging gear with a big bump on his head lying on the grass verge. The young man who had found Damian said; 'As a car drove along a door flew open and a body rolled out into the gutter. The car did not stop but drove off at high speed.'

Damian struggled to sit up. 'No, it was a van, a huge van full of old ladies and they were hitting me with books.'

The police officer looked at the paramedic and tapped his head.

'Concussion!' He whispered

Damian heard him. 'No, no, there were hundreds of them all screaming and swearing.'

'Old ladies you say? That doesn't sound like old ladies' behaviour. Why would they attack you?'

Damian felt the bump on his head.

'I'm not nice to them I suppose.'

The police officer named Jim, smiled in the darkness.

'Well I hear many explanations for being beaten up however, I have never heard of old ladies being the perpetrators. This nice man will take you in his ambulance to the hospital for a check-up. We'll follow and take a statement and perhaps by then you can come up with a more plausible reason as to why anyone would attack you.'

As Damian was being stretchered into the ambulance, Jim said to the man who had phoned for help.

'In cases like this it's usually to do with drugs or if they have upset other gang members. Did you see any old ladies in a van?'

The man thought hard.

'No, I only saw the lights and the body roll out. It was very dark, and I was more concerned for the person on the ground. I have no idea if it was a car or a van. The poor chap was rambling when I reached him.'

The next week Joyce again went to the book department with her new novel.

'Do I need an appointment to see Mr Billinghurst?' she asked the spotty assistant.

'No since his accident he has gone back to the old system. I will tell him you are here and then bring you a coffee.'

Joyce smiled thinking wait until I tell the girls

Spooky Wedding Day

It was my favourite cousin's wedding day. Arriving at the old church on a bitterly cold day under glowering, dark and threatening skies, we fought our way in horizontal winds up to the church porch. Hector furling his umbrella that had proved useless in the fierce gusts, remarked that the omens for this tying of the knot were not looking good.

I laughed nervously and seeing my Aunt Augusta turning to greet us, forced a bright smile. 'Hello Auntie, how are you? This is Hector my fiancé.'

Aunt Augusta had always terrified me as a child and was no less forbidding now I was grown up. She was tall and leant heavily on her walking stick. An ex headmistress of an upmarket girls' school she treated relatives as if they were disruptive pupils sent to her for misbehaving. She was surrounded by a choking smell of mothballs and her usual shapeless navy-blue dress with its pleated skirt and modesty inset neckline never changed. However, it being a wedding, on her head was an enormous concoction of feathers and flowers stuck on top of her iron-grey hair that was pulled back into a tight bun at the back of her head.

Turning her Sparrow Hawk gaze to Hector, she looked him up and down as if he were a small boy in short trousers with dirty knees. Could she not see how handsome he was with his lovely grey-green eyes and curly chestnut hair?

Her face softened, 'Very nice.' She said and with the hint of a wink, she led the way into the church.

'Bride or Groom?' Chirped the usher, reminding me of Ed Sheeran. 'Bride'. We replied and walking towards the front of the pews, we settled into the second row between my sister Eve and a distant but not distant enough cousin called Penelope.

We had only just made it as the Wedding March rang out from the not very in tune church organ. There was much craning of necks as the congregation turned to see the bride enter on the arm of her father. Moonbeam, an unfortunate name thought up by my Aunt Jessica after too many Green Goddess cocktails looked radiant. Blond, stick thin and pretty to a ridiculous degree, Moonbeam was a vision in her oyster hued satin, figure hugging, full-length dress with a six-foot train held up by two adorable page boys. Several small bridesmaids followed in pink dresses with floral coronets on their heads. One did not like her coronet and flung it on the ground. Her mother rushed forward, and a hissing conversation followed until chocolate was mentioned and peace returned.

As Moonbeam passed our pew, I marvelled at her violet eyes and rosebud mouth looking ghostly behind a gossamer veil.

'Lucky so and so. Amazing how a title can lure a girl even to a chinless wonder like Monty.' Muttered a losing swain sitting behind us. Obviously, goodwill was not on his moral compass today.

The vicar was young and only in charge as the older and permanent vicar had succumbed to a bout of salmonella after eating a dubious sausage roll at a WI party.

The fledgling vicar's entire contribution was conducted at a rapid rate as he nervously fingered his hymn sheet. At the exact moment Toby, the Best Man was to produce and hand over the ring an owl with the ring in his beak was swept aloft by his handler from the back of the church. This unusual and very expensive touch had been Aunt Jessica's response to her arch-rival, Tracey whose daughter Pandora had been married two weeks earlier. Hell hath no fury like a bride's mother in the bridal equivalent of climbing Everest.

Suddenly, just as the owl took to the air the storm broke. Thunder crashed, lightning flashed through the many stained-glass windows in blinding glory. The owl dropped the ring and with wild screeches flew straight at the vicar. Showing dirty trainers beneath his flapping cassock the vicar legged it to the vestry.

The panicking owl flew at head height round and round the church for what seemed like ages with the terrified congregation ducking and screaming. Hats were lost including Aunt Augusta's as the owl grabbed the feathers from its crown. Several young girls had hysterics until the flying missile finally answered his handler's desperate calls and returned to his gloved hand.

'I am not paying for that.' Muttered Aunt Jessica as Tracey smirked.

With the ring recovered, the service resumed after the vicar emerged sheepishly from the vestry. Moonbeam was now Lady Moonbeam de Quincy and another marriage was done and dusted.

'Now for the good bit, I'm starving.' Hector whispered as we all trooped off for the reception.

Rachel and Rosie - The Party

The rather sleazy man in a dropped stitch jumper was showing Rachel around. The stitches had come undone where the moths had bred their young and caused the ladder like pattern.

'My name is Mr Octavius Plimp.' He said, as he led the way up the stairs to the first floor of the newly finished and furnished house. 'I have been given the job of resident janitor by Mr Crosby. He runs the biggest building firm in this town,'

Mr Plimp obviously thought Mr Crosby was a very important person. Opening the second door along the landing he stood back to let Rachel pass. She was pleasantly surprised. The room was bright and had new carpets and furniture. It had that just delivered smell and the one window let the light flood inside.

Going over to the window, she looked out at the view of the small close. Copper Beeches, the name of this house was on the curve of the close with four largish houses on either side.

'The site used to be a public house and restaurant but closed several years ago. Mr Crosby demolished them and built these houses. He had earmarked Copper Beeches, being the biggest, for himself, but his wife Estelle did not think it was grand enough. So that's why he is letting it out as separate rooms.'

Rachel nodded thinking Estelle was mad, I would kill for this house, well of course not literally she thought but fixed Mr Plimp with her hazel eyes and said, 'Do the tenants have a kitchen?'

'I will show you, follow me.'

As they went down the stairs, Rachel noticed Mr Plimp had trouble negotiating them and held tightly on to the bannister rail. Opening a door off the large hall, it revealed a fabulously appointed kitchen that contained every conceivable modern appliance.

'Very nice.' Rachel realised this was the understatement of the year.

There is a rota of names that list whose day it is to keep the kitchen clean.'

Rachel stared at the names, Rosie, Mia, Emma and Ruby. Mr Plimp obviously was the type who thought domestic cleaning was not men's work. Next, they discussed the rent, which seemed very reasonable.

'I would like to take the room please. When can I move in?'

'Right away, this is the last room and I already have someone else who rang up after you who is interested. One month's rent in advance.'

Luckily, Rachel had her chequebook with her and wrote the cheque made out to Crosby Holdings and handed it over. Mr Plimp gave her a key to the front door and filled out a rent book. After thanking him, she left feeling relieved. Since moving down from her hometown in the Midlands to work for travel agents in the town she had been sleeping on the sofa of a friend from uni.

Later that day she had moved her few possessions into the room and stared round with a big sigh of satisfaction. On the pale pine dressing table were ranged all her makeup bottles and pots and an antique box that held her few items of jewellery. The white fur covered stool was great to sit on in front of the dressing table mirror and her clothes were hanging neatly in the built-in wardrobe.

'Bliss', she said out loud, collapsing onto the single bed covered with the floral duvet and matching pillowcase that she had just purchased in the town. Two minutes later, she was fast asleep.

There was a knock on the door and Rachel came back to consciousness, wondering for a minute where she was. Then got up and opened the door.

'Hello, I'm Rosie. Have you time to talk?'

'Of course, do come in, I was just catching up on my sleep after some rather disturbed nights.'

Rosie was young, pretty, a bit plump, with long light brown hair and an infectious smile.

'I have the room next to you and I heard you talking to Plimp on the landing earlier.'

Rachel laughed, 'Is that what you call him?'

We all do. He is a bit odd and he has the room the other side of yours.'

By now, Rosie had seated herself on the fluffy stool and Rachel faced her perched on the end of the bed.

'Tell me all the lowdown about who else lives here. I mean are they nice and what should I be careful about?'

Rosie took a deep breath. 'Well first there is Mia, she is from Sweden and very pretty. Next is Emma, a bit wild and funny. Then Ruby who can be a bit sharp and tells it as it is, she doesn't take any old buck from Plimp.'

'Is that it?' Rachel smiled at Rosie; she already felt that she had found an ally in this much younger teenager.

'Not quite. On the next floor, which also has a super bathroom with one of those huge corner baths, there are two guys. Hugo is very strange, he's autistic but a whizz on the internet. He only comes out of his room when we are all out. Next to him is Kenny, he moved in last week, so we don't really know anything about him except he's a jobbing actor.'

'Why are they not on the cleaning rota?'

'Believe me they will be. You wait until Ruby gets cracking; she is one for her rights.'

'What do you think is a jobbing actor, Rosie?'

'I have no idea but that is how Plimp described him. I think it means he is out of work more than he's in work.'

Rachel now had a picture of the setup. 'Thanks Rosie, I'll go down and get my bearings. I had a big lunch today, so I am not hungry and tomorrow I will buy some food.'

'We write our names on anything we put in the fridge, today you can help yourself to any of my stuff.' Rosie smiled and stood up. 'I have a job in the evenings at The Five Bells pub, as I am still a student and it gives me a bit of spending money. See you later.'

How nice to have a fellow conspirator already, Rachel thought, as she went down to the kitchen. There were three girls sitting on high stools at the breakfast bar. As she entered, they stopped chatting and smiled. One gave her a very quizzical up and down look.

The pretty blonde who had a smile that would melt snow said, 'Hello you must be the new tenant, Plimp said we now have a full house. I am Mia and this is Ruby next to me and then Emma on the end.' There was a slight broken accent in her soft, throaty words.

Ruby glanced up from stirring her coffee and waved an airy hand, 'Hi, what's your name?'

'Rachel.' For once, she could not think of anything more to say.

'Well I never, Ruby, Rosie and Rachel, the three R's. I will enter you on the rota pronto. Mia, Emma and I were just talking about the party we are planning for next Saturday. As it's our party and we have done all the organising, as a newcomer you can only bring one guest, same as Rosie.'

Rachel felt like telling Ruby what she could do with her party however, she smiled and nodded. 'Fine, thanks, I think I'm free that night.'

Emma, who was stick thin with long tawny hair and a perfect oval face, smiled showing her very white teeth.

'Take no notice of Ruby; her bark is worse than her bite. We were just discussing whether we could come up with a plan to head off Plimp who comes down in his tatty old dressing gown every night at precisely ten o'clock for his late-night cocoa. He then sits here drinking it sometimes for ages. That won't add to the sophistication of the event.' Emma let out an infectious chuckle and winked at Rachel who joined in the laughter.

'How about giving him a glass of Champers and putting a couple of sleeping pills in it. That should send him off to the land of nod early.'

'Now then Ruby we don't want to finish up in a police cell for janitor doping.' Mia was obviously the responsible one of the group. 'I will appeal to his better nature and ask him to stay in his room.'

'Well good luck with that.' Emma said as she stood up. 'I have a soap to watch. 'Nice to meet you Rachel.'

With that, the girls drifted off to their rooms, leaving Rachel to make a cup of tea and familiarise herself with where things were in the kitchen.

Back in her room, she gazed out of the window. A fascinating scene caught her attention. Outside the house on the right-hand side, an elderly man with military bearing was loading two large and snappy Chow dogs into the back of his Land Rover. After lifting their front legs up into the back of the car, he then lifted their back legs in as well. This rewarded him with a painful nip on the arm. That's gratitude for you. Rachel thought as the man drove off to no doubt give them a walk in the local park.

Someone coming out of the house on the left-hand side caught her attention. A well-preserved and fashionably dressed woman emerged and got into a white Rolls Royce, the car door held open by a man in a chauffeur's uniform. Rachel recognised the lady immediately as Tamara Browne who had been a quite famous actress and film star. Her many affairs and marriages had kept the gossip columns going for years, alerted always by Tamara herself. The driver also had a familiar face. Rachel searched her brain and then came up with the name of a bit player from Tamara's last play in the West End. Jack Miller, at least thirty years younger than her. Rachel remembered how, sitting in the audience she had laughed, as everyone but Tamara had red noses and looked frozen, whereas Tamara glowed pink. She obviously had the only warm dressing room and had made sure the rest of the cast froze, thus making the younger cast look washed out.

Next morning Rachel awoke and gazed at the tea making device sitting alongside her on the bedside table. It was supposed to have automatically boiled the water, syphoned it into its teapot and produced a lovely brew. Today it had decided to do nothing, and she once again had her daily battle with it and its unpredictable temperament . Occasionally it worked as it should and the cup of tea it produced was lovely however, most days the red light came on but nothing else happened. Once it had disgorged boiling water but not into the teapot, leaving a big puddle for her to clean up. Frustrated she banged it and it coughed into life and started to hiss. She lay on her side watching until at last it had made a pot of tea which she poured into a cup and drank gratefully, she had put a couple of Earl Gray teabags in the pot, so no milk was needed.

It then only took her ten minutes to wash at the small wash hand basin in the room, apply her makeup and throw on the navy business suit and striped shirt, her work place uniform.

After walking the short distance to the railway station Rachel caught the train for the two-stop journey to Waverly Bend, the town where she worked. The travel agents were part of a large chain and employed three female sales staff and one male manager, who were all smartly dressed in matching trouser suits, and sat behind large computers on the top of pine wood desks.

Rachel, being the new girl had the desk at the back of the shop where the brochures were ranged in racks behind her and she spent a lot of time picking them up off the floor. She didn't mind this, as with her Travel Agent's degree in the desk drawer, knew it was only a matter of time before she rose up the pecking order and would finish up at the front desk.

As the new girl she also got the first slot for lunch, this suited her as not having had any breakfast she was starving. There was an independent snack bar next to the shop and Rachel had exchanged jokes with the owner, a young man from Poland with a great line in dry humour.

'Fancy coming to a party on Saturday?' Rachel said, as she picked up her ham roll and coffee.

'Tell me the time and address and I will be there.' he said as he handed over her change.

Rachel wrote down the details on a white napkin and smiled her thanks.

'It's a Castaway fancy dress party. That means any tatty old gear will do and rip it up all you like.'

'Sounds fun, thanks, I'll see you there.' He went back to dealing with his next customer.

Back at the Holiday Company shop, Rachel settled herself behind her desk and studied her fellow workers. In charge was Warren, a rather weedy thirty something, with thinning hair which he compensated by growing it long at the back. Not a good look she decided.

His mother Edna was on the payroll but for what reason Rachel could not imagine, as her contribution was nil. If a customer approached her desk Edna's expression was one of terror. When they wanted to enquire about a destination and what holidays were available this meant looking it up on the computer. Edna had never mastered anything to do with computers, so the customer was passed on to Warren, Joyce or lastly Rachel. Edna would beetle off to the back office and make herself a cup of tea until it was safe to come out again. When management visited, Edna would take a day off, so they were unaware of this bit of dead wood.

Joyce was the perfect description of smug. Although exceedingly drab and plain, in her eyes she was wonderful. Never having been known to give a compliment or remark on anything that did not concern her or her clingy daughter, she dispatched her husband when it became clear that it was more profitable to divorce him and get the house and the poor man's savings.

'I didn't want to cook him his meat and two veg anymore.' she would say when asked why she had divorced him. Her obsession with money was all consuming. When it came to a bonus for selling holidays, she would knock other staff out of the way in her efforts to be top sales and get the money.

Later, back at Copper Beeches an amazing sight met her gaze as Rachel looked out of her window. In the garden of the house on the right-hand side a woman in a pink, boned corset with dangling suspenders and nothing else was standing by the rockery. Eventually, the Colonel, as Rachel now called him, came out and gently steered her back indoors.

While still standing at the window Rachel saw Tamara Browne emerge into the front garden to pick up her tiny pet dog who had made a dash for freedom. Jack Miller could be seen at the front door and was being torn off a strip for not stopping her handbag size dog escaping.

'You useless idiot. Jason could have been run over. What do you think I keep you for?' Tamara's perfect diction carried as if it was a first night and Rachel was in the stalls.

'You know what you pay me for Honey,' Jack drawled. 'But I have had enough of your tantrums.'

With that, he slammed the front door leaving Tamara still holding Jason to knock repeatedly on her own front door.

What drama goes on here Rachel thought and went down to the kitchen in the hope of Rosie being there. Only Emma was in the kitchen eating beans on toast with a fried egg on top.

'Hi Rachel,' Emma paused, a fork full of beans halfway up to her mouth. 'I was famished. Help yourself to the rest of the beans in the saucepan I have had all I want.'

'Thanks Emma that is nice of you.' With that, Rachel scooped the beans on top of the muffin she had bought earlier and pulled up a chair next to Emma at the large kitchen table.

'About the party', she said her voice muffled with beans. 'I asked a chap I know if he would like to come and he said yes, so that's my guest sorted. How are the arrangements going?'

'All under control. We've ordered the finger food and wine from the supermarket who will also supply glasses, Kenny is going to set up the music with the help of an actor friend from the local repertory company. The only fly in the ointment is Plimp who so far refuses to give up his nightly cocoa in here, however, we live in hope that he will change his mind.'

Rachel nodded, 'This house is brilliant for a party, and I can't wait for Saturday to come. Who are you bringing Emma?'

'About ten people and one special guest that is a secret.' Emma let her chuckle hang in the air accompanied by a wink.

'What kind of job do you do? I bet it's something glamourous.'

'If you call being a foot slave glamourous that's me. I work in a Beauty Salon, but I do all the pedicures and reflexology appointments. If I never see another naked foot, it will be a relief. I trained for two years in all beauty treatments but the dragon that runs the salon never gives me anything but feet. I am looking for a man to take me away from all this.'

Rachel smiled, 'Well good luck with that. How did Plimp finish up as janitor here? I mean what is his connection with Mr Crosby?'

'He's one of his site foremen and with a dubious past and no fixed address. Mr Crosby saw Plimp as a needy case and has tried to help him. I personally think Crosby is wasting his time. Things have gone missing from our rooms; I would count your underwear if I were you, as we have all lost things.'

Rachel's eyes were like saucers. 'Crikey, that is awful. What an odd setup and of course, as we can't lock our doors anyone can get in and go through our drawers. What about Kenny and Hugo, have they lost things?'

'Not so far, but Plimp asked Kenny to his room for coffee and he said Plimp has a glass topped coffee table with very suggestive pictures underneath the glass. Kenny made his excuses as soon as possible and fled. As the rooms and house are great we all keep quiet, but you have been warned.'

'Thanks Emma, I've never come up against a situation like that before, what a sleazy character.'

There was a cough behind them and Plimp, in his slippers and dressingown, limped in and silently made his cup of cocoa, then sat on one of the high stools, stirring it noisily. Had he heard? Rachel thought as she and Emma put their plates in the dishwasher and left Plimp slurping his late-night drink.

Upstairs, Rosie was just returning from her stint behind the bar at the Five Bells pub. 'How did it go?' Rachel asked, pausing as she opened the door to her room.

Rosie pulled a face. 'Ghastly, everyone orders a round then they all change their minds and order something different and I have to try and remember. If I didn't need the money I wouldn't bother. But I do so I grin and bear it.'

'Tough choice but we are all on our own, so jobs matter... Good night Rosie, sleep tight'.

Rosie blew a kiss followed by a yawn. 'Good night Rachel, I will.'

Saturday evening arrived, and the house was transformed into a sea of noise and colour. Music boomed, and laughter bounced off the walls, Rachel had found a large fur muff in a charity shop and with Rosie's help had transformed it into a furry bra by passing two lengths of cord through it and tying them at the back. A beach wrap from a summer holiday tied at her waist and some shell earrings completed her castaway look.

Rosie had covered herself in spray tan, sewn artificial flowers on a crop top and slashed an old pair of yellow trousers into ribbons. 'I think we could pass as a pair of rather exotic castaway maidens.' Rachel said, as they stood back to look at themselves in the mirror.

'Let's go down and see who's turned up.'

The sight that met them was riveting. A swirling colourful melee of people, all ages, most unrecognisable in their fancy-dress costumes as castaways. The music shook the very walls of Copper Beeches. The wildest dancer was a tall man in torn trousers that left nothing to the imagination, a long, matted wig and his face covered in charcoal made any features a mystery.

'Who is that?' queried Rosie as Emma twirled past with of all people Jack Miller.

'No idea but meet my special guest.' Emma laughed, 'Tamara is hopping mad.'

'And meet my new girlfriend.' Jack said as he gazed adoringly at a radiant Emma.

'Well, I didn't see that one coming.' Rachel said, as the pair danced away into the sweating throng. Tomas appeared looking quite respectable in a cheesecloth shirt and torn jeans.

'I didn't have time to get any fancy dress. What a great house and a great party.'

'I am so glad you made it.' Rachel smiled taking his hand, 'let's get a drink.'

Rosie's date, Josh, a boy she knew from working at the pub arrived dressed as Long John Silver, complete with a stuffed parrot on his shoulder. 'My Dad runs a fancy dress hire business.' He said by way of explanation, as he executed an uninhibited exhibition of Dad dancing.

'Did he teach you to dance as well?' Rosie laughed as she joined him dancing to the strains of Come on Eileen.

Precisely at ten o'clock Plimp appeared in his faded plaid dressing gown and ignoring all around him made his cup of cocoa. He then sat on one of the high stools, drinking it noisily.

'I knew he would.' Muttered Ruby to Kenny who was Disc Jockey for the night. 'I hate him, and he is a dirty old man.'

Kenny nodded, 'I told you he showed me some suggestive pictures when I went to his room to pay my rent. Why is it that if you are an actor everyone thinks you're gay?'

'Search me.' Ruby said as she scowled at the oblivious Plimp.

'Please,' laughed Kenny. 'Now what is your musical request Ruby?'

How about Killer by Michael Jackson that's how I am feeling.'

At that moment Hugo appeared with a large pair of scissors and went around snipping at everyone's slashed Castaway outfits to make them even tattier. Unfortunately, he cut straight up the back of the new shirt worn by Tomas who took a swing at Hugo landing a punch on the side of his chin.

'Ruddy idiot, I only bought that shirt today and it was very expensive.'

'Well how did I know that, you foreign lowlife.'

Hugo's chin was bright red, and Rachel could see this was about to escalate. 'I need another glass of wine Tomas, and you Hugo make yourself scarce.'

Rachel led the way to the bar in the kitchen just as Plimp stood up and put his empty mug in the dishwasher.

The crowd of dancers parted like the Red Sea as Plimp then silently made his way up to his room.

Hugo had disappeared and with a glass of wine in their hand, Rachel and Tomas leant against the bar.

'I am sorry Rachel, but I do have a short fuse. My life before I came to England was very rough; my instinct for self-preservation takes over before I know it.'

Rachel stared at him and realised there were several scars on his handsome face that she had never noticed before. 'I do understand Tomas, Hugo is a very odd person so try to forget that incident. I don't think anyone else noticed.'

'We did,' Mia said as she and a very handsome man came up to them. 'Take no notice Hugo is weird. This is my twin brother Sven who is working in the A and E department at the local hospital here while he completes the last year of his Doctor's degree.' Sven was the exact male equivalent of Mia, the same blonde hair and dazzling blue eyes.

'Lovely to meet you.' Rachel shouted above the music and thought no wonder the hospital is extra busy with a gorgeous medic like Sven working there.

Sven shook hands and smiling down at her said, 'Perhaps we can have a dance a bit later on.' Lost for words Rachel nodded and the heavenly twins then disappeared into the crowd.

It was well after midnight when someone noticed water dripping through the ceiling of the second floor. Ruby was first up the stairs to the top bathroom and let out a piercing scream. Kenny and Sven followed, and a terrible sight met them. A body was lying submerged in the large corner bath, which was overflowing, with bloody water. It had covered the floor and seeped through to the bathroom below.

Sven turned off the taps and released the plug, so the water started to drain away then after checking for a pulse he shook his head. 'Someone ring for the police this man is dead,'

'My God it's Plimp.' Gasped an ashen-faced Ruby and promptly fainted into the arms of Sven while Emma ran in and dissolved into hysterics. Jack led her away as Kenny took charge ushering onlookers downstairs.

Within minutes, two police cars with their blue lights flashing pulled up outside and several uniformed officers and two men in plain clothes rushed inside.

'Good morning everyone my name is Detective Inspector Holland, and this is Sergeant Harris, first of all no one must leave the premises.

'Holland and Harris, they sound like a firm of tailors.' Muttered Josh hoping to lighten the mood slightly as Rosie was in tears.

'I know I didn't like Plimp, but this is terrible.' Rosie sobbed. 'I have never seen a dead body before.'

Josh tried to give her a hug although the stuffed parrot got in the way.

DI Holland addressed his men. 'Sergeant you stay by the door, no one is to leave, and the rest of the team take everyone's name and details. Harris you come with me.' With that, the detective inspector addressed Kenny who was standing nearby, 'Please take me to where the victim was found.' The DI had seen many murder victims, but this was something else. The soaking wet shape of Plimp lay on the bottom of the now empty big corner bath, the blood, a vivid trickle edging its way down to the plughole. A pair of scissors embedded in his chest and the tasselled cord from his dressing gown was tied tightly around his neck.

'Whoever did this made sure he wouldn't survive. I'll phone the photographer and the pathologist so after they have done their work we can move the body. You stay here Harris and I will go and see how the name checking is progressing.'

Downstairs one of the police officers was taking Ruby's details.

'Name please.'

'Ruby Rose.'

The young sergeant sighed; it had been a long night.

'I want your surname for the record.'

It was Ruby's turn to sigh as she said wearily. 'Rose IS my surname, so my whole name is Ruby Rose.'

'Thank you. Next person please.'

As Jack went up to the police officer recording the information, she just stopped herself from asking for a selfie after recognising him from interviews on television. Rachel then moved into the seat he had just left next to Emma.

'Emma darling, do tell me about your romance with the gorgeous Jack.'

Emma rolled her eyes. 'Yes, he is stunning, isn't he? We bumped into each other when he was walking Jason that piece of knotted string that is Tamara's prized pooch. It was one of those things, instant thunderbolt attraction. Anyway, he was fed up with Tamara and her silly ways and luckily he has been given the lead in a big new television series to be filmed in Spain.'

So, if he's in Spain what happens to you?'

'That's the good bit. Jack has wangled me a job as a makeup artist on the film. Isn't that just dandy? No more feet.'

'Wonderful, I'm so pleased for you.' Rachel smiled and squeezed Emma's hand. Then found she was next up to give her name.

Meanwhile, upstairs the photographer was packing away his equipment and the pathologist was carrying out an initial search of the body.

'What have you found?' Asked DI Holland entering the bathroom where the pathologist, an attractive redhead, was on her knees beside a limp Plimp.'

'He was stabbed between his second and third rib with these scissors which were open at the time and left two deep wounds however, I think the victim's death was caused by both the dressing gown cord being tightened around his neck and finally being submerged in the bath.'

'Well whoever did this did not want him to survive. Ah, here are the paramedics; he's all yours boys.'

Plimp was loaded onto a stretcher and taken down the back stairs to a waiting ambulance.

Joining his team on the ground floor, DI Holland addressed the assembled partygoers.

'Can you remember if there is anyone who was at the party who is not here now?'

Puzzled faces searched their tired minds, and someone called out. 'That tall bloke with the terrible long wig.' There was a murmur of agreement.

'And Hugo is not here.' Kenny said, 'I haven't seen him since that bit of trouble with the scissors.'

'Scissors!' DI Holland's eyes widened behind his spectacles, but he did not comment. After checking that all the names and details of those present had been recorded, he continued, 'everyone but the residents can go now however, please do not leave town. The people who rent rooms in this house I want you to remain where you are. Thank you everyone else for your help.'

As the deflated partygoers filed out, he said to Harris, 'You take everyone in the team outside and search the garden; we have two missing people who attended here for the party. A tall man that no one can put a name to and a resident called Hugo. I have called the dog handler and he should be here any minute.'

Just then, the dog handler called Bruce arrived with Boris, an enormous German shepherd dog. Together they were famous throughout the force as they always got their quarry.

After filling Bruce in with the details, Bruce and a bounding Boris disappeared into the garden, which was dotted with flashlight beams. Minutes later, there was a scuffle and furious barking from Boris. Hugo had been found hiding in the remains of the wine cellar that was once part of the now demolished restaurant. Hugo was a sorry sight, dirty and shivering.

'Good work Bruce and Boris. Your reputation is further enhanced.' The DI then turned his attention to Hugo. 'Now firstly confirm your name and then explain what circumstances led to you hiding in the garden.'

Hugo's eyes were focused on the floor and when he spoke, it was hardly more than a whisper. 'I came to go up to my room and as I passed, the bathroom the door was half open. I could see a man with my scissors in his hand, shouting at Plimp. The man was still in his fancy dress.'

'So, what was this man saying?'

'That Plimp was a thief, that he had sold material and equipment from building sites and falsified accounts... Then he lunged at Plimp with the scissors and they fell against the door, which slammed shut, so I ran down the back stairs and into the garden, I was scared the man would see me. I had come across the remains of the cellar when I was looking for quiet place to read in the garden.'

DI Holland nodded encouragingly, 'Did you recognise the man?' The DI's voice was quiet, realising he must not scare Hugo into silence.

'Yes, he was still dressed in his castaway outfit, but I knew the voice. It was Mr Crosby.'

There was an audible intake of breath from the girls and Kenny, who said. 'Hells bells, there goes our landlord.'

'Can you describe how he was dressed?'

'He was covered in charcoal and had on a long, matted wig which was slipping sideways.'

'He was the mad dancer. I think he had gate crashed the party so that he could confront Plimp.' Rachel whispered to Rosie.

'Thank you, Hugo. We will take you to the police station to give a written statement. Harris, I want you to go to Mr Crosby's home and bring him down to headquarters.' DI Holland smiled round at the remaining partygoers. 'Thank you everyone, I think that is all for now. I will wish you good morning and let you know any outcome of tonight's event.'

As the police trooped out, Ruby surveyed the dirty glasses, spilt wine and scattered debris of the party.

'We will tackle all this tomorrow.' She looked at her watch. 'I mean later today, much later. That sure was a party to remember.'

BV - #0010 - 240119 - C0 - 210/148/7 - PB - 9781912243525